The Sidekick and The Supervillain

Super Love, Volume 1

SE White

Published by SE White, 2022.

THE SIDEKICK AND THE SUPERVILLAIN

First edition. September 17, 2022.

Copyright © 2022 SE White.

ISBN: 979-8201792848

Written by SE White.

Table of Contents

Chapter One

MICHAELA'S SECRET IDENTITY turned out not to be so secret at the urgent care facility where she worked. Now she had to figure out how to swear him to confidentiality or she'd lose her job. The most annoying thing about it all was that The Evil Bane had done it. A supervillain with a name like *that* had no business being smart enough to figure out her alter-identity.

"You're the sidekick," he repeated, black eyes narrowed. "The one with a name you need a thesaurus for." He snapped his fingers, redirecting his gaze to the ceiling as if the words he needed were printed there on an encouraging cat poster. *Hang in there, sick friend. My alter-ego is the Amiable Accomplice! You're in good hands.*

"You're always with Furia. I'd swear you're her sidekick. Wait, I'll remember in a minute," he insisted. "I think that shot you gave me is kicking in and making me forgetful. My arm feels better, though."

You're always with Furia...

Michaela breathed through the lingering pain of that one and ignored the supervillain. If he thought he'd get another chance to see her fighting beside The Fabulous Furia he had another think coming. Her days of trailing along as the world's most useless sidekick were over. Twin jolts—one an ache, one hurt pride—stabbed through her, and she chased them off with a slight shoulder shake.

She bustled around, avoiding his eyes while she laid out sterile gauze packs, sealed saline bottles, the glove boxes, and large gauze pads in case they had to debride his wound. Instead of speaking to him, she brought up his charts on the computer system.

The Evil Bane didn't require another person to keep a conversation going, though. He rambled, trying different alliterations, but she tuned him out. He was no more interesting than the training dummy she'd practiced on to get her Licensed Practical Nurse certificate.

1

Okay, a flabby rubber dummy didn't have those rock solid abs. Dummies didn't have luscious, tuggable sable locks. Seriously, what brand of conditioner did he use? But the principle stood. He was no more than a really good looking patient.

"Let's check your blood pressure," Michaela said cheerfully. She slipped the Velcro cuff over his uninjured arm, carefully avoiding those deep, dark eyes. He obviously thought she'd help him shatter her cover voluntarily, maybe if he smoldered enough.

"The Cordial Caretaker. . ." he tried. "No, the Affectionate Amigo? *Oww.*"

She caught his glare from the corner of her eye. Delicately, she adjusted her fingers so she wouldn't touch any part of his skin while she held the diaphragm to listen to his artery close and open. Her nitrile gloves slid greasily along her fingertips with every tiny adjustment.

For one scary second she had to fight down an unfamiliar urge to rip the damn suffocating gloves off and just *touch* the world around her like any other being.

"Does it really need to be that tight? I mean, really?"

Michaela angled her head away so she could get away with changing her expression. Rolling eyes was forbidden bedside behavior—even when you were treating The Evil Bane. She released the pressure, listened, then finally took the dreaded torture device off of his arm.

Then she left all common sense, training, and reality behind and stripped off her sweaty, constricting gloves. *With a patient close enough to touch.*

Tossing them in the trashcan gave her a slightly terrifying thrill of triumph.

Chapter Two

IF SHE THOUGHT ABOUT the sin she was committing she'd freak out, so instead Michaela focused on entering patient stats.

"One-twenty over eighty," she muttered, finding the right entry in the laptop sitting open on the counter.

You took your gloves off what are you doing *your gloves are off!*

"One-twenty...over..." there was the correct spot. She tapped it in before the numbers left her head, fighting the urge to flex her shamefully bare fingers. Then she leaned closer to peek at the pulse oximeter capping his slender forefinger. O2 Sat hovered at ninety-six so no worries there, but his pulse fluctuated wildly. "And one-oh-five. Hmmm."

"What?" The Evil Bane peered at her suspiciously. "What *hmmm*?"

She finished entering his heart rate without answering. Anxiety built and built until her brain screamed with it.

Gloves you have to be wearing gloves you can't touch him put your gloves back on!

"You said two different numbers back to back. Is that normal? Am I normal? What does that mean, Kindly Comrade?"

Somehow Michaela forced herself to stop chanting *gloves you can't ever take off your gloves!* internally and focus on her patient. "There's nothing to be worried about," she told him. "One-twenty over eighty was your blood pressure. That's completely average."

He pinched his lips, appearing faintly insulted.

"And your heart rate is" —she watched the monitor jump from one hundred and five to one hundred, then back to one hundred and one— "a hundred and five beats per minute. That's a bit faster than normal, but you *are* in urgent care. People often have an elevated heart rate under stress. It's all common. Don't worry." She dug a new pair of gloves out of her front pocket and tugged them on in defeat.

He tried a grin. It wasn't his usual, cutting, evil-genius grin. Not the one she remembered seeing as he traded banter with Furia. "Okay, Benevolent Buddy. If you say so."

She barely restrained a snort. "Sir, I think you have me confused with someone else." *Benevolent Buddy.* "Let's take another look at your arm," she suggested.

"Oh, no. No, thanks. Let's not look."

Michaela tilted her head to the side. "If you won't let me look at it, the doctor is still going to anyway."

"Could she not? Or he not? Whoever. Just not. Could we just numb me up really good and send me home?" He flashed the hopeful half-grin again. But he kept his gaze carefully away from the scorched, weeping furrow high on his left bicep.

"With possible contaminants in the wound? So you can get infected and have to come back?" She gave him a gentle, yet impatient look. The same look Fabulous Furia gave Michaela whenever she asked to come back her up in a battle. "If this wound gets infected, you'd have to come back and the doctor would have to *cut it back open* to let all the pus drain."

He winced and shifted on the narrow hospital cot.

"After we cut it back open we'd have to irrigate it," she went on, merciless as winter air over a frozen river. "That means flushing it over and over to get the infected material out. *Then* we'd have to *scrape* away the dead tissue, which is called debriding, with a tiny toothbrush-looking thing and try to dig out any pockets of—"

"Ooo-kay!" He waved his good arm in emphatic *stop* circles. "We don't need any more details." His mouth twisted into a sour curve. "You can look at it."

Grinning, she stepped around the cot to his side and leaned forward. She'd kept insisting. And she'd *won*. It was a first for her.

"But don't touch it!" He jerked his neck and head away.

"I won't touch it," she said. He might be one of the most skittish patients she'd ever seen in here. When he relaxed a touch she couldn't resist adding, "The doctor will."

As she examined the burn she leaned closer, careful not to touch. Even with nitrile gloves on she had to be cautious. And anyway, he'd asked her not to. "What were you doing? How did a burn give you such...slashed edges?"

Burns typically had a rounded shape, originating from the contact spot and spreading out. This looked like he'd somehow gotten sliced with an incredibly hot knife, cauterizing as it cut. Overall the laceration was fairly small, maybe eight or nine centimeters long, but it looked nasty. Even with the Lidocaine, it had to hurt.

He muttered something in response. Sounded like *spearmint*.

She tilted her head up to ask what he meant and she was only a breath, the barest touch away from that gorgeous face. He looked so kissable at this distance. She had to tamp down a surprising urge to nip his full lower lip before she kissed her way up to those sharply defined cheekbones—*No, Michaela. Bad, Michaela.*

He'd been leaning over to watch her as she examined his wound—*not* thinking about kisses. She lurched back a step and tilted her head away.

This time he gave her a *real* Bane grin. Cocky, overconfident, sexy as all hells. She'd never known the color of his eyes or how amazing his bone structure was, not through the obnoxious Evil Bane mask he wore. But the mask only covered the top half of his face. She'd always thought he'd left it like that deliberately to show off that handsome square jaw, because yeah, he knew he was handsome. And oh, she knew that seductive grin.

Without her approval, her traitorous insides fluttered and her mouth turned up in an answering smile.

"I've got it," he said abruptly, his eyes lighting up. "I remember. You're the Amiable Acccom—"

She straightened her hand flat in front of his nose. "I am not *the* accomplice, or *an* accomplice, or an amigo, or a buddy. I really think you have me confused with someone else. I need to ask you to stop, sir. You'll get me in trouble." Darting over, she peered out the small window in the examining room door.

Dr. Imark was approaching down the tiled hallway, shoes tapping on the tiled floor. Michaela had seconds.

She dashed back, leaned closer, and lowered her voice. "Everyone knows you can't trust Empowered to work in a hospital. They might accidentally hurt someone or attract a villain. Everyone *knows* that. Please, Bane. Let's just focus on your injury."

Their eyes locked. He looked unconvinced and she *could not* have that.

Normal Michaela instinct hunched her shoulders, muscles twitching in preparation for turning away. She refused. This job was important to her. Everything in her needed to stay, to help people, and for that she *had* to keep her status as Empowered a secret.

"Please, Bane. Just forget what you think you know." Her heart boomed in her ears once, twice, three times. Everything shrank to the two of them, bolted together, waiting to see who would break first.

Finally, he gave her one tiny nod.

"What do we have here, Michaela?" Dr. Imark's big, booming voice entered the room even before she did.

Sound and color flooded back into Michaela's peripheral, like someone had hit the button to un-mute the room around them. She blinked and tried to focus, grateful the pulse oximeter wasn't on *her* finger.

"Ahhh...oh, it looks like...a deep partial-thickness burn. Combined with some laceration." She pointed at Bane's wound, avoiding his gaze once more. "Some edema at the edge of the burn here. Blistering here and here, see. Patient's blood pressure is normal. Heart rate a little elevated. I already gave him a topical shot to numb the area but we might want to give him one more."

"And who are we treating today?" Dr. Imark gave The Evil Bane a friendly smile as she moved to the sink to wash her hands.

"Ivan," Bane told her. "Ivan O'Reilly."

Michaela snorted involuntarily and clapped a hand over her mouth. She had skimmed right over that part of his chart. His abs had been a tad distracting. But of course he wouldn't check into the facility all barefaced under his evil name.

Ivan O'Reilly. Her side twinged from holding in the laugh that fought to burst out.

He looked like the furthest thing from an *Ivan* or an *O'Reilly* and of course that's why he'd chosen it as his alter-ego.

Both of them stared at her, Doctor Imark with amazement and Bane with one side of his mouth tucked up. His cheek dimpled, which she considered deeply unfair to females and fems everywhere and herself in particular. She dropped her hand to her side and calmed her expression.

"All right then, Ivan, let's get you fixed up," Dr. Imark said, giving Michaela a *do-you-need-to-go-on-break-now* look.

Behind Dr. Imark The Evil Bane winked and Michaela gave him an unimpressed look, even though she could feel the heat of a blush brushing her face.

Chapter Three

HIRO GRITTED HIS TEETH and tried harder to ignore the pounding ache. The shot had helped. Some kind of topical anesthetic goop around the edges of his burn eased the pain even more. Dr. Imark had been as gentle as she could. But the ghost of agony still haunted his entire arm, crawling through his bicep, creeping up his spine to make him twitch.

Pain had never been something he handled well. He loathed shots. Hated hospitals. Avoided the dentist like a bop concert with glitter cannons. Even though he hadn't watched The Amiable Accomplice and Dr. Imark patch him up, his imagination had taken over and his stomach squirmed at the mental images of what they'd been doing to his arm.

And that lecture about scraping off dead tissue. Ugh. She knew damn well how gross it sounded and she'd used it against him without a qualm.

She was so pretty. And so underhanded. His very favorite combination.

Of course he couldn't trust his nurse. The Evil Bane trusted no one. And she'd done something to him. It had to have been her. Hiro flexed his fingers. For a second–no, the breath of a second–his hands had felt wrong. Out of nowhere, he'd had this terrible *urge* to put gloves on, to cover up his skin. *Gloves?*

Even stranger, the feeling had nothing to do with him or what he'd been thinking at the time. It had been foreign, separate, intrusive. And he had a strong suspicion it had to do with the sidekick treating him.

What exactly were The Amiable Accomplice's powers? No one had ever said specifically. He'd never seen them on a superhero blog or listed on one of those obnoxious talk show segments. She didn't even exist on a wiki list and it only now occurred to him to wonder why that would be...

He caught her checking out his bare chest again and smirked, stealing another look at her nametag. *Michaela.* The Amiable Accomplice was named Michaela. Immediately, she shifted her eyes to scowl at the bandage she was holding and lifted her chin up, pretending he hadn't caught her doing anything. The queasiness rocking his stomach settled a little.

Who would have guessed the Amiable Accomplice worked at an urgent care facility? And why was he even surprised? Superheroes had a *saving-people* thing. Of course they'd do it on their downtime too, even if it was frowned upon.

He thought of her wide eyes and pleading expression when he'd figured it out. She really hadn't wanted him to know.

Please, Bane.

He wanted to hear those words again. Exactly those words, but with a different inflection. A naked inflection. A *please, Bane give me more* kind of nuance. When that gorgeous black hair was spread out all over his pillows and he was in the middle of exploring every centimeter of smooth skin. And those big eyes were wide with pleasure, instead of worry.

She'd called him *Bane.* She knew who he was—his villain identity, anyway. He'd only come up against Fabulous Furia and her sidekick twice over the last five years. The Amiable Accomplice had mostly been kept in the background, watching him trade blows with her superhero while she kept his bots busy. But she still recognized him.

Hiro was never going to complain when a pretty girl remembered his villain identity. Even if she ran alongside one of the most self-righteous superheroes in the city.

"—how it happened?"

"Hmm?" Hiro tore his eyes away from his nurse. Again. "I'm sorry, what?"

The Doctor gave him a dry smile, her brows lifted. "I said, did you have any luck remembering how it happened? It's an unusual burn."

I'm for damn *sure not admitting in front of Michaela The Amiable Accomplice that I was testing laser-eye-proof glass and didn't check the angles before I fired and the laser ricocheted back on* my own arm.

He gave the Doctor his best sunny, sincere, open look. "I guess I just wasn't paying attention when I made my toast this morning."

"Toast," she repeated.

"The toaster gets really hot. Those edges are killer. I knocked into it and it was going to fall off the counter and I think I panicked a little. Tried to nudge it back with my arm. Clumsy."

"The toaster did it," she said. The absolute flatness of the Doctor's voice made it clear, she was not amused. "So it wasn't, for instance, a deadly new type of weapon your employer might, as a random example, have you testing out?"

The fight not to let the insult show on his face was strong, but all internal. Alright, so he didn't actually have any minions and had to do all his own testing. Still. Assumptions hurt.

In the far corner of the room, where she was carefully disposing of the bloody pads and towels, Michaela's shoulders shook. When she glanced his way her eyes sparkled with the laughter she struggled to keep bottled.

"I would *never* work for one of those terrible, evil villains," he said primly. True, in the most literal sense. Minions would be working for *him*, someday. "It was the toaster."

"Sure. Okay. Dastardly little things." Dr. Imark shook her head. "We'll have to watch out for more toaster injuries. Well, you're all set to go, Ivan. You've got your discharge papers?"

He tapped the sheaf of papers he'd dropped at his side and nodded.

"And you know what you should be concerned about?"

"Any increasing pain, any seepage through the bandages, swelling, and any dizziness, fever, vomiting, or nausea." He reeled it off and made a face. Vomiting was possibly his least favorite thing in the whole world, and that included all the superheroes in Smallcity.

"Alright then. See the receptionist to check out on your way to the door. And come right back if you feel concerned about anything. Don't forget to pick up those antibiotics." She made her way to the door, already tapping away at her tablet, most likely checking details for the next patient.

"Thanks, Dr. Imark," he said.

She waved a hand in his direction and disappeared.

Hiro didn't know how they did it, these good people. Working to someone else's schedule eight to ten to twelve hours a day. And whiny patients demanding things for every one of those hours, bodily fluids everywhere, barely enough pay to justify any of it. *No, thank you.*

He flicked away those thoughts and smiled over at the resident sidekick. He'd never guessed before today that one of his kinks would be Sexy Nurse, but he was definitely into those ankle length scrubs. "So, your name is Michaela."

She crossed her arms and gave him a flat stare.

"It's on your name tag," Hiro pointed out helpfully.

"Unfortunately, it's a policy," she said, scowling at the tag. "I thought about getting something less obvious like, *The Amiable Accomplice, TOTALLY not in disguise as your nurse, have a nice day.*"

Real appreciation flavored his laugh. "When do you get off work, Michaela?"

The smile in her eyes snuffed out. "No."

"I didn't even ask yet."

"Still no. Supervillains and sidekicks don't mix."

"They could." He winked at her.

"But they don't. Opposite sides, opposite goals. You hurt people for a living, Bane."

Her voice wobbled and her shoulders rounded protectively. But she kept her chin up, looking him right in the eyes. The contrast, on top of all her other mysteries, only interested him more.

"Only a little." Even as the words left his mouth he knew it was the wrong thing to say. Too nonchalant. "I'm more in the line of providing...things to people who need them. Not hurting people."

"The things you provide kill people."

Irritation wiped away any traces of his smile. "I have *never* killed anyone. Or provided anything that does."

She lifted both brows in a look which clearly stated, *bold claim*, and shook her head. "Bane, you're charming, and funny, and really good looking. But this is not happening."

Edging his way off of the crackly thin paper of the table, Hiro sent her an ironic look. She couldn't have realized—being told he couldn't do something always fired him up to do exactly that thing.

Challenge accepted.

"I'll be seeing you," he warned. And with one last considering look over his shoulder, he left.

Chapter Four

A BOUNCE OF PRIDE STILL lifted Michaela's step as she walked out of the employee entrance at the back of the urgent care and into a bright afternoon. Today the whole world looked fresh and bright and perfect. The sky flowed in rich summer blue. Even the robins perched on the scrubby bushes lining the parking lot sounded cheerful to her.

She didn't know if it was the fact she'd been at work, or she'd felt particularly brave yesterday, or what—but she had stood up to The Evil Bane. A *supervillain*. They'd actually butted heads. And she had won.

It felt even *better* than the battle, so long ago now, when Furia had complimented her hand-to-hand combat with Doctor Nasty's minion.

Even in her secret life battling crime as a sidekick Michaela got along with everyone. She'd actually *apologized* to a minion she'd knocked down in a fight, once. That's why she was the loyal sidekick, not the superhero. Starting conflict was not her forte. Her civilian social life? Always zero drama or conflict. Always.

The first word people thought of to describe her was quiet. *Amiable.* With a father who was the most famous superhero in several galaxies and a mother whose power overshadowed Michaela by a factor of ten, what other option did she have? There wasn't room for three alphas in their house. Michaela had learned early that she'd better sit down and say *yes, sure, whatever works for you,* all day every day if she wanted a happy home life.

But she'd told Bane *no*. She'd looked him right in the eye. Something about him made her feel confident enough to do it. Maybe that slow, easy grin. Or maybe it was his uber cocky attitude. He told bald-faced lies without even blinking and said whatever he wanted to without worrying about people's opinions. Somehow, Bane made her feel unsettled and brave, all at once.

Such a shame I had to turn him down. But, a sidekick and a supervillain, that's just begging for trouble. With a big bright neon target

13

on both of your backs. She sighed and cracked her bag open to start searching for the car keys.

A newly familiar voice spoke from beside her. "You get off at six. Good to know."

Michaela gasped, spun on her heels, and thrust her hands out in front of her, ready to yank off her gloves and *push* out some power. A lean, masculine form stood in the concealing edge of the leafy bush she'd parked next to. The robins perched in the branches chirped away, madly unconcerned they were about to be caught in a battle.

Both of them froze for several seconds. Then Bane straightened out of his own defensive crouch. His smile bloomed. "I come in peace."

He bowed and, with a flourish of petals, a bouquet drifted out from behind him. She swallowed. *Right. He has potenkinesis.* He floated the flowers through the air until they were right in front of her. "And bearing pretty flowers, for the lady."

Michael nibbled the inside of her lip. He looked so damn sexy in black pants and a charcoal gray shirt. And with a burst of flowers dancing in front of his fingertips...so tempting.

As she lowered her hands, she shook her head. "Bane. I did say no." She couldn't decide if her heart was racing because Bane stood *right there*, because he was giving her flowers, or because she'd been about to touch him with her bare hands. Maybe everything combined.

"I just love a challenge." He waved his empty hand theatrically, drifting the flowers closer to her.

"I didn't give you a challenge." Despite wanting to bury her face in the blooms, she ignored them and went back to fishing out her keys. They were so cute and colorful, a little rainbow of gerbera daisies with fat, cheerful petals. "I said supervillains and sidekicks don't mix."

"Ah, that's the challenge. They could mix." He grinned at her and nudged her free hand with the bouquet, soft petals tickling against her skin. "Not professionally. I'm not *that* silly. But socially. I could be your dirty little secret."

His voice went lower on the last few words—right into the danger-to-Michaela's-sex-drive octave. The idea was enough to warm her in a flash from the inside out. He'd be the *best* kind of dirty secret. *No, Michaela. Bad, Michaela.*

She surrendered, turned her hand over, and grasped the rough stems of the flowers. "Thank you for the flowers. They're beautiful. Now go away, Evil Bane." They gained weight in a sudden rush against her palm as he released the bouquet from his power.

He wiggled his eyebrows suggestively at her. "I'll just be back tomorrow."

She couldn't help but smile. He was so adorable. And oh, Powers, he had a squared jaw. An. Actual. Square. Jaw. He was practically *designed* to make her all mushy inside. If only there was some way they really could do something about this sparking, electric attraction. It might be worth the trouble he'd cause...she sighed. No. It would never work.

Her mother would *never* forgive her if she started dating a supervillain.

"Don't you have, um, sharks to strap some lasers on? Computer squirrels to train? A brace of minions to whip? Something?" she asked him.

Bane clapped a hand to his chest and staggered back a step. "I'm wounded. The thought of not hearing another comeback like that, it wounds me right in my villain's heart. You wouldn't deprive me of this wonderful sparring. You've already figured out my devious plot for the squirrels."

Well, he *was* fun.

He stepped forward again, edging closer. "I'm great company. I'm funny. I'm all intriguing and mysterious and dark and stuff. I will brood, upon request." He pouted in a super exaggerated way, eyes dancing, the opposite of brooding and somehow even more attractive. "And going on dates with me would be an *excellent* way to rebel a little against restrictive parents. When's the last time you did something rebellious?"

Never. I've never dared, never rebelled over anything. She buried her face in the flowers to hide her wide grin. The sparks jumping through her from head to toes could easily become addictive. He was so handsome. And so dangerous. In twenty-two years, she'd never guessed how enticing that combination could be. Maybe—maybe this could happen. If they were careful. If she was ready to ignore some of the rules and *risk*.

She peered over colorful petals at the supervillain standing in front of her. "Bane, I want you to tell me something. And I want you to be truthful," she said. The flower stems slipped against her clammy fingers. Fighting a lifetime of being quiet and unassertive took gut-scrambling effort.

He straightened his face into a serious look and raised his right hand, three fingers up, thumb and pinkie folded together. "I will tell you something. And I'll be truthful. Unless you ask me my real name or the location of my lair."

She rolled her eyes and didn't bother to hide it.

"Sorry," he said. For the first time in the entire conversation he sounded sincere, without any hint of humor. "I should have thought before I said that. Of course you'd know better than to ask something so obvious. I'm ready. Go ahead."

"Have you ever killed anyone?"

He rocked back on his heels and his head tilted. "You pull no punches with these first date interviews, do you?"

"It's important to me." She kept her eyes on his, fighting the instinct screaming to look away, to back off.

"I've never killed any civilian," he said seriously. "I never will. That kind of world dominion shit is not my goal."

She believed him. His voice, his body language, the expression in his eyes—he meant it.

And he felt so strongly about it that she could see a hint of it in the air without even touching him. This happened sometimes when people were focused on one emotion hard enough. He didn't know she had the ability to see it, so he wasn't trying to block off his emotions.

"And superheroes?" She hugged the bouquet closer to her chest.

"Ah. Well. That's different. They pick fights with me all the time." He tucked his hands into his back pockets and scuffed the toe of his shoe against the ground in a little circle. "I've never killed one, though, if that helps. Just kind of beat them up a little. Please, Michaela? I'd really like to take you out for a date."

I can't believe I'm going to do this. If mom ever finds out, I'm in so much trouble. But, if she could speak her mind so fearlessly to Bane, perhaps she could start speaking her mind in other parts of her life, too. Maybe if she spent enough time practicing around Bane she could start walking with a bit of his swagger, inject some of that confidence into her own grin.

And he was freaking attractive.

She raised her chin to look him straight in the eyes. "Yes."

Those eyes widened. "Wait, yes? I don't have to beg? I was all prepared."

She shook her head, letting him see her smile. "No need. The other supervillains would kick you out of their club."

"Yeah, well, keeping myself on the mailing list for that super-boring newsletter is not worth giving up a possible date with you."

Her heart stumbled, just a little. He was joking, he had to be, but that was still the sweetest thing anyone had ever told her. "You won me over with your stalking in the bushes and the flowers," she said. "I'll meet you tomorrow. It's my day off."

"I wasn't stalking, I was waiting. Behind a bush," he muttered. Then he brightened up. "Where?"

"You know the pier, in Ocean City?"

"Yes."

"Meet me by the arcade there, at 1:00." It wasn't so hard, *speaking* assertively. She wasn't as sure as she sounded, though. What if he was busy? What if he'd been kidding about wanting to see her so badly? What if she was walking right into some kind of incredibly complex plot?

Using his power he tugged on a strand of her hair, gently, from three feet away. "I'd have to move 'whipping the minions' up on the schedule...but I can make it work. I'll see you there," he said.

One little empowered tug on her hair made her whole spine light up like an ecstatic LED strip.

"Okay" she breathed. *This is defiant. Incredibly not like me.*

His grin spread and grew. "Okay" he agreed. With a wink, he stepped back around the bush and was gone.

Chapter Five

THE PIER IN OCEAN CITY thronged with people enjoying a warm, late-spring day. It wasn't hot enough to drive them inside yet. Perfect carnival weather. A salt-filled breeze tugged at Michaela's loose hair while the sun caressed her shoulders over the thin spaghetti-straps of her dress.

She inhaled the smell of fresh popcorn, the sugary tang of cotton candy, the heavy grease from frying food. Clangs, buzzes, and chirps from the festival games filled the air while their tiny lights flashed pale against the sunlight. Today was going to be fun.

Here she stood, being rebellious. Doing exactly what she wanted, with a date *she* had chosen for once. And that date was The Evil Bane. It might be stupid and reckless but she was *tired* of doing everything right all the time. In that spirit, she'd worn her thinnest gloves today.

A light tap on her elbow made her whirl around.

Bane stood several steps away, looking entirely unrepentant. A white silk rose hovered near her arm and, with a flick of his hand, floated up to her eye level. It was one of those cheap, gimmicky mementoes sold only at carnivals, with a tiny spray of rainbow lights bursting from the tips of the petals. She *loved* it.

"Bane, you have to quit sneaking up on me." Michaela released the glove she'd been preparing to yank off and looked around to see if anyone had noticed the reaction. Her heart thumped wildly against her ribs and she wasn't sure if her panicked build of power or his cute gesture had caused it.

"Thank you." She plucked her new flower out of the air.

He tilted his head to indicate her gloved hand and raised a brow. "If that comes off, are you going to blast me with...ice? Shoot web nets at me? Laser-palm me off the pier?" he asked. "You look wonderfully retro today, by the way."

She let out a laugh, enjoying his shameless attempt to wiggle information about her powers out of her No Empowered being in the city, besides her family, knew her exact powers and she sure wasn't about to discuss the details now. Definitely not with The Evil Bane. Keeping them secret was second nature.

She shook her head and started down the boardwalk. Bane fell into step beside her.

Even though he'd listed of a lot of terrible things her powers might do to him, he didn't look particularly worried about her actually doing them. She eyed his unassuming charcoal gray shirt and wondered what sort of gadgets he'd hidden in the cloth fibers. Under the edge of his left sleeve the bandage she'd helped put on him at the urgent care peeked out.

"Ready to go on a ride, Bane?"

His eyes glazed over a little and he gave her a wistful look. "Say that again, only really husky, you know what I mean? And while you flip your hair in the breeze." He demonstrated with a sassy head toss.

Laughing, she nudged his good arm with hers. "Shut up."

The slight buzz of a dormant force field tickled against her elbow. She pursed her lips, genuinely impressed. If he'd worked out a way to link a personal field to a normal looking shirt he had tech skills she'd never suspected. And she'd seen his tech in action, holding off the Fabulous Furia and her firebombs. It was extraordinary.

He quirked one shoulder up into a half-shrug. That dimple reappeared with his crooked smile. "Where would you like to go first?"

"Somewhere that won't stress your arm, so no bumper cars," she said and started off towards the Ferris Wheel dominating the end of the pier. She took a few steps, realized he wasn't following, and turned to glance over her shoulder in silent question.

"That's...really kind of you to remember." He looked quizzical. As if he wasn't used to people noticing or caring enough to make allowances for his injuries.

As a supervillain—he probably wasn't.

Her heart smarted a little, because it was a sucker when it came to probable emotional damage, the daft thing. "I'm not going to be the reason you burst a stitch and have to go back to see Dr. Imark."

He laughed as he strode forward to catch up with her. "All Powers forbid. She'd chuck a toaster at my head."

Michaela joined in his laughter. The whole day seemed sharper with him walking next to her. The carnival stood out in crisp color; crowd sounds faded to become their own background. She couldn't quit watching the way the sunlight caught the edges of his dark hair or shake the image of her leaning in to kiss that dimple on his cheek.

They took their time examining the booths until Michaela decided on the shooting game. At first Bane took the place next to her, blasting away, but when she hit everything she aimed at he abandoned his own toy pistol to hover behind her.

She darted a suspicious look over her shoulder.

His face gave away nothing. "I want to learn from the master, here."

She turned back as the next row of cardboard villains popped up. His closeness vibrated along her entire back. She made her first shot, but then warm, soft lips pressed against the back of her neck and her second went wild.

She dug her teeth into her bottom lip, hard, to fight back the delighted smile and focused on the dancing targets. Despite three more distracting kisses, five in the row flopped over. She took half a second to turn and toss Bane a challenging look.

"Mmm. I have to try harder, don't I?" He was pressed so close his voice rumbled through her in the worst, most delicious way.

Michaela shivered. Contrarily, the more he tried to divert her, the more she wanted to hit every target dead on. So she let the shiver tremble from her head all the way to her toes and then tightened her grip on her little plastic pistol. The next row, this time alien villains, slotted into place and she started shooting.

She let burst three shots and two targets flopped over. Then his lips brushed the curve of her ear and the whole right side of her body tightened. *Oooh* he was sneaky. Her points climbed higher as she moved along her row, knocking targets down. But before she could take her last shot his teeth closed gently on her earlobe and she jerked so hard it hit the top corner of the booth, high above the range. *Damn it.*

She dropped her gun so it dangled, forgotten, off of its plastic cord as she whirled around and slapped a gloved hand across Bane's chest. Her breaths panted much faster than a pretend shooting game at a carnival deserved.

He had his cockiest Evil Bane grin on, so she lifted her chin and told him, "I still won."

His arm curled around her to fold them tight together. It seemed like the natural thing to wrap her arms around his waist in return.

"I know you did. Your concentration is as impressive as your aim, Amiable Accomplice," he whispered. His breath puffed lightly against her temple, stirring her hair, and she fought down another shiver.

For one second, stretched long and sweet as taffy, she stared at his mouth so close to hers and wished hard for a kiss.

Then the game attendant cleared his throat. "Um. Um. Your toy? Uh, did you want it?"

She forced her attention off of Bane to look at the poor teenager, whose cheeks were a painful looking pink. A tiny stuffed purple hippopotamus slumped on the counter in front of him. He coughed uncomfortably and nudged it closer.

"Right. Thanks." Heat washed over her own cheeks, but Michaela took her winnings and gave the teen a brilliant smile. Bane buried his face in the curve of her neck and started laughing.

She shoved him with her hip. "Oh, move, you terrible terror."

"Okay," he wheezed.

He let go of her and they started down the aisle of games again. Her whole body tingled and missed his touch. Apparently she'd left all of her common sense at the end of the pier. And oh, none of this could be the smart way to do things but she'd never felt this free with anyone before.

"Here." Michaela extended the plum-colored stuffy to Bane. Purple, the same color as her super suit. It seemed very appropriate.

"Really? You won it."

"So I can give it to whoever I want, and I want to give it to you. Thank you for my rose."

He took it with a pleased smile and tucked it into his pocket.

At the ring bottle game they played next he missed every single one of his tosses, even though Michaela stood there, too shy to try and distract him the same way he had. Instead, he made her snort with his running commentary about the crowd.

Later, when he exchanged cell numbers with her, her heart kicked. No, it actually *leapt*, as if she had somehow fallen into a random timehole and landed back in high school.

They bought crispy, indecently greasy corndogs at the food booth and he used his potenkinesis to knock an extra-persistent seagull off the wooden railing of the pier in a flurry of feathers. It fluttered right back to peck at their crumbs.

By the time they reached the line for the Ferris Wheel, Michaela knew she had tripped herself right over her own stupid, reckless impulse and into a blazing infatuation.

Chapter Six

HIRO LIKED WOMEN—THE way they looked, the way they moved, the way they smelled. He didn't have as much of a social life as he would have liked, maybe, but he made time for occasional dates and enjoyed all of them. He appreciated the different experiences but they didn't leave what he'd call a *deep connection.* They all ended exactly the same—a few dates, some pleasant kisses, the possibility of more for a night, and done.

He didn't know how, but Michaela was already...*more.*

More fun, more exciting, more of a challenge, more addictive. Maybe it was the thrill of dating someone from the other side. Possibly she was just too gorgeous and overloaded his system. Maybe it had just been too long since his last date. But it absolutely could not be that he was infatuated with her. Of course he wasn't stupid enough to be falling into feelings. This was their first date!

He caught her looking at her rose again, smiling tenderly. The tiniest sting pricked his heart, opening up a little hole for a sweet ache to nest in.

NOPE, he thought at the foolish, soft feeling. *Not doing it. Don't even start.*

The line inched down the pier, closer to the giant Ferris Wheel looming above them. Hiro avoided looking in the direction of the top. He'd be fine as long as he didn't look over the edge.

He'd just look at Michaela instead.

The next two people got on the contraption, letting Hiro and Michaela step forward. Hiro eyed the swinging seats and the rickety looking spokes holding them. Why did it have to be so high? He'd worked hard on conquering his acrophobia, but it would never go away completely.

He and Michaela reached the front of the line. Subtly, he hoped, he peered over the railings into depthless, shadowy blue water. They'd survive a fall. If they managed to hit the water instead of the wood. Probably. Hopefully. *See? You'll live.*

He stared hard at the tiny motor box at the center of the enormous wheel, letting his *instinct* for electronics pry inside. Every single component ticked along cheerfully. To his enhanced senses, all the cogs meshed and all the belts spun smooth. In the time it took to breathe in once, his power snaked along every wire in the circuit. All of them were fine, running uninterrupted with the correct current.

The contraption might be terrifyingly tall, but it was safe. Some of the tension constricting his shoulders eased. He'd be surrounded by electronics the entire time the damn giant thing lifted him high in the air, and gadgets were *always* under The Evil Bane's control. They'd be fine.

Michaela bounced on her toes as she give the attendant their tickets, clutching her rose in the other hand. Her hair cascaded down to the center of her back, a beautiful dark contrast to her pale skin and flowery blue dress. Wearing a bell-shaped skirt, sensibly heeled sandals, and white kid gloves, she looked like a chic lady who'd warped to the present from a 'Support Your Superheroes' bake sale in 1952. She was so damn happy to be here. He couldn't ruin it.

He made sure to sit on the inside of their nasty, yellow aluminum seat and fixed his gaze hard on the horizon. The motor ground into gear and the big wheel started turning. Oddly enough, clutching his purple hippo released some of the strain.

He darted a quick look at Michaela. "I think I'll name him Blight," he said.

"What?" She turned away from examining the expanse of glittering ocean surrounding them. Soft spring sunlight framed her hair. It highlighted those wide cheekbones, traced along her straight, slim nose, outlined her pointy little chin.

Every thought of the endless space beneath them left his head.

"Who's named Blight?" she prompted him.

"Huh? Oh." He glanced down and waved the hippo, vaguely. "My buddy here. It goes well with Bane, don't you think?"

"Definitely."

He leaned closer, giving up any resistance to the call of those pink lips curved into a smile. "Michaela, I'd really like to kiss you."

She caught her lower lip between her teeth, considering, and his heartbeat wanted to stutter. "I'd really like that, too."

"Thank Powers." Closer, closer.

He cupped her face with one hand, used his thumb to trace lightly over her bottom lip. Soft flesh curved against his finger as her smile widened. Her eyes drifted shut just as he drew near enough for their breath to mingle. Over the tang of ocean he smelled something citrusy, something sweet. Michaela.

He brushed their lips together, softly. Once, and then again. Even the briefest touch shocked through him like he'd bumped a live wire in the lab.

She was so soft and giving. He kept the pace slow, testing and teasing. The Ferris wheel spun upwards, making him feel weightless, and his heart leapt with it, soaring. Her little sigh brushed against his mouth as her hand cupped the back of his head.

They deepened the kiss, tongues exploring together. Kissing Michaela was another experience to add to the definition of *more*. More slick heat, and continuous sweet pressure. He wrapped one arm around her waist and pulled her nearer, pressing their thighs together. Close enough to feel the heat of her skin press against his own, but it still wasn't close enough. Maybe she'd like to sit on his lap while they forgot about everything else in the world for a while.

He tightened his arm, ready to pull her up and over him. Something *boomed*, rudely jerking his attention away from the woman in his arms.

"What the *hells*—"

Underneath them the Ferris Wheel groaned and shuddered. Their seat lurched to the side and Hiro's stomach seemed to go with it.

Chapter Seven

MICHAELA BROKE THE kiss and her eyes flew open. When had she moved so close to Bane? She was practically in his lap. Her heart galloped along at giddy, breakneck speed. His arm tightened around her waist, a firm brand burning through the thin material of her dress.

If he shifted his fingers an inch he'd brush the underside of her breast. Heart, mind, and body—*definitely* her body—all yearned to lean forward and nip at his lower lip again, to keep diving into that sweet, sweet tension and ignore anything else. She'd never been kissed so blind before.

But a lifetime spent around battles informed her: that boom just now had not been a good noise.

The ride had stopped with their seat at the highest point. Because of course it had. She'd barely noticed, what with all her nerves getting melted off. The bleached wooden boards of the pier below them looked impossibly far away.

The crowd flowed and tumbled, a determined mass surging back towards the land-end of the pier. No one panicked because they'd all been through battles before. The key was to figure out where villain and hero were fighting and go the opposite direction. And hope no powers surged unexpectedly, hurting or killing bystanders. There were shouts, the occasional high-pitched scream rising above them.

Something flashed at the edge of her vision. She twisted to follow it. Bane's hand tightened on her side.

Leaping back and forth, jumping from waterspout to wave to pier and back was—Water Wonder. Of course. She could just make out his dark hair on top of the signature teal blue super suit. Clearly, he was in the middle of an intense battle.

His opponent seemed to be—she squinted harder—Sea Bitch. Dark purple tentacles and sweeping blue hair darted through the chaos of waves.

28

Seriously? They have to do this right now. She glared down at the wrestling combatants. *All Powers damn their timing.*

Riding a frothy wave, Water Wonder roared up and over the edge of the pier and crashed into the mechanical base of the Ferris Wheel. The whole structure shivered and Michaela grabbed at the railings around her. Enormous tons of metal structure had just *moved* and knowing that fact sent a nauseous shiver all the way to her toes.

Bane let go of her to grab onto the metal rail, his face drawn and pale.

Sea Bitch pursued the superhero, using her tentacles to rocket into a vicious attempt at a full-body hit. He dodged, of course, and she *slammed* into the wheel herself.

Michaela wanted to scream at them, although they wouldn't hear over their fight. Even if they did hear they wouldn't understand her, or care. Superheroes battled supervillains. Time and place didn't matter, only stopping Evil did. Of course Michaela wanted Good to prevail but couldn't, perhaps, *both* sides think about prevailing somewhere not crowded with innocent civilians?

The wheel lurched again and their bucket jerked and dropped. Michaela's guts plummeted. A baby screamed somewhere, and a man shouted. She gripped the metal railing tighter, trying to get her bearings.

"I think. The ride. Stopped working," Bane squeezed out.

She turned to look at him. Every bit of color had drained from his face. His grip on the railing was so hard his knuckles had turned white.

She reached out and stopped short, her gloved hand hovering uselessly in the air above his arm. The instinct to help him was so strong her fingers actually shook. She curled them into a fist, her glove sliding around her skin. *No one* liked it when she used her power. It creeped them out. She'd learned not to even try.

But his panic shouted clearly in every tense line of his body.

"Looks like it did stop working," she said, as calmly as she could manage. "Water Wonder and Sea Bitch are battling down there. I think they broke the motor, slamming into it."

"Of course they did." His lips twisted, but he still didn't open his eyes. A wealth of unexpected bitterness seeped through his tone. "When did superheroes ever care what they broke?"

She tilted her head sideways. That sounded like an *issue*, one for another day. She shelved it for later. Right now, they had to fix the fact that they were stranded in a crumbling ride high above the pier.

"Bane, can you float yourself down? Are you strong enough?"

"To lift a whole person? No. I can move small things." His voice shook.

She yanked her hand back, finding it only inches from touching him. Again. The drive to use her power thrummed through her veins, stronger than ever before, but she *couldn't*. "Okay. It's okay. Um, maybe we could climb?"

Leaning over, she assessed. The battle had moved further into the carnival. Bits of games went splashing into the water left and right. Cheap plushie toys, Blight's relatives, floated sadly atop the waves. The fair-goers in the bottom few buckets of the Ferris Wheel were bailing from their seats to make a dash for the safe end of the pier.

Still locked at the top of the ride, Michaela had a perfect view of everyone beneath them. The higher two-thirds of the wheel had plenty of people trapped, too high to climb. People of all ages, alone or in family groups, cried out for help. Panic rose in a grayish white mist, so clear Michaela could hardly believe no-one but her could see it. Two buckets down a mother clutched a crying baby to her chest. Her face turned up towards Michaela with a helpless, despairing expression.

They had to do something.

"Bane, we have to figure this out."

"I can't. I can't move."

"You don't have to," she soothed. She eyed the mechanism at the base of the ride. "You're good with mechanical things, right? I've seen some of it in action."

Metal *groaned*. Could her own fear be causing her to imagine the wheel lurching to the side a little? Or was it really damaged?

Bane grabbed her thigh with his free hand and squeezed so hard it stung. His other hand hadn't left the rail. "Michaela, this is bad."

"Mechanical things, Bane. Focus with me. If we can climb down somehow—"

"I'm not moving. I can't. I can't climb."

"Acrophobia?" she guessed.

"Really bad. This is, like, the worst case scenario."

"It's okay, Bane. We're going to figure this out." Her calm tone wasn't doing enough. She *itched* to lay her palms against him, to chase out his panic.

"I have an idea," she said.

"I'm listening."

"You said you can move small things. Can you focus on the motor down there? Maybe get it moving again?"

He opened his eyes, finally. "Maybe? I'd have to look at it and visualize what kind of motor it is, picture the components in my mind to move them." His intense, dark gaze never wavered from hers.

"But you can't look down."

"But I can't look down." One darting peek was enough. He jerked his eyes back to hers and licked his lips. A light sheen of sweat coated his face.

She reached out. "Bane, I can help you calm down. I can help you look."

The wheel lurched sideways, sliding her across her plastic seat. No denying the slant as her imagination now.

"Please, Bane. Let me calm you."

"Is that, like, your power? Making people calm?" He sounded sincerely fascinated.

"No, not really, that's only part of it. Please! We have to try," she urged.

"Alright," he said. "Try."

Before he got out the "y" in "try" she'd tugged both gloves off and dropped them by her feet. She slid the few inches between them to lay both palms against his bare right arm. On the inhale of one long breath, she reached deep inside to collect the feelings she wanted. *Calm. Centered. Peace. Quiet.*

Using the power came as simple as breathing to her. It always had. She *pushed* everything through the contact point of their bare skin. *Calm.* Her feelings became his, as his cycled back into her. For a moment, dizzying vertigo tried to take over. *Centered.* She took the panic, his hot, blinding fear, and shoved it away. To her it looked like flashes of jagged white lightning. She sent it flickering out, shining once against the deep blue sky and then gone. *Peace.* No fear allowed here. Instead, she fed him cool, green confidence.

He jerked and took a deep breath of his own. "Wow."

"Look down," she said quietly. "Can you see the motor?"

Smoothly, he leaned over to peer down. She absorbed the jolt of renewed panic, took away the spinning, dizzy sensation of falling. The more seeds of calm she planted in him, the more he grew and fed them back to her, an endless, sustaining loop. Her heart rate slowed, her breathing evened out. *We can do this. You can do this.*

"I see it. Let me try to get the motor running again." He reached out as his brows drew into a grimace of focus. "Yeah. I think all the banging jarred some stuff loose. There's a—yeah, there's a backup battery for the motor. I think it's a hydraulic motor. Feels like it, anyway."

They sat locked together by the touch of her hand and the link of her power. Michaela tuned out the crashing coming from the still battling Empowered, the shrieks of disturbed seagulls, and the occasional shouts, to focus on the supervillain trying to save them.

Bane had his eyes narrowed at the tiny metal box so far below. Michaela kept her palms pressed against the skin of his forearm, smoothing her hands up and down in slow, gentle waves.

"Bad news. No motor," he said finally. "It's too broken. Too many little parts crushed to get it working."

Tendrils of panic tried to creep into him again, like miniscule, choking white vines. *No! I'm in charge. Go away,* she thought at it, and poured even more energy into her calm. To her eyes Bane appeared to be outlined in a pale green mist. He looked like a science fiction movie with a decent budget.

"How does the wheel move? What parts do the motor move to get this wheel spinning?" she asked. Part of her envisioned gears all moving together like the inside of a clock.

He leaned into the fragile metal bars caging them, trying to get a better look. Their plastic bucket rocked back and forth.

"Huh. Tires," he said. His surprise washed over her, a brief tint of yellow. If it *was* his...their connection was so strong she struggled to distinguish which emotions were hers and which belonged to him.

"What?" She followed his gaze but couldn't tell which part of the wheel he was talking about.

"Car tires." He turned his head to smile at her. That dimple appeared.

Too late, she remembered their link. She had totally just sent him the bolt of lust that ripped through her. *Damn it. Michaela. NOT the time right now!*

His smile turned positively sly. *Triple damn it.* "Car tires?" she prompted.

"It's a kind of friction roller. The motor turns the tires, and the tires force the wheel to move."

"Um, that sounds unlikely, but okay. Can you turn the tires without the motor?"

"Yes? Let me try." He held both hands out. Determination bled from him, a navy-blue rope so strong it made *her* sit up straighter.

His shoulders started shaking. All she could do was *push* more willpower to him. *We will do this. You can do this. We're getting down from here. No one's going to die today.*

The Ferris Wheel *screeched* and jerked forward a little. People below them screamed. But it was moving. Three buckets forward, then four.

"Stop," she said.

The wheel quit moving. Michaela leaned forward and cupped a hand around her mouth. "On the bottom, get out! Climb out!" The other hand stayed on Bane, feeding him the calm they both needed to live through this.

After the bottom few buckets were emptied, Bane focused and moved the tires again. This time he groaned with the effort. Through Bane, the heaviness of the wheel overwhelmed her. The effort it took for him to move it tore through her. How much more did the force tear at *him*?

Finally the wheel rotated enough for a new set of people to escape safely onto the pier. When Bane let it halt, she didn't like the way he panted, or how his forearm shook beneath her fingers.

We can do this. We're going to get down from here. No one is going to die today.

"One more time," she said. "Just one more. You've got this, Bane."

This time, the pier was much closer. The climb wouldn't be the easiest thing she'd ever done, but she didn't think Bane could move the wheel again and she wasn't going to ask him to.

The mother she had seen earlier carefully handed her baby down to a woman who stood safe on solid wood. After she scrambled out, she looked at Michaela, who had both hands wrapped tight around Bane's forearms in their bucket, still three levels above safety. Michaela jerked her head at her, *Go!* The little family took off running.

Safety Patrol had arrived. Their lights scattered red and yellow reflections against the frothy tips of the waves, and their sirens blared. The carnival magic was gone, only twisted metal and sparking wires left flickering in the sunlight.

She squeezed Bane's arm. "Ready to climb down? Let's get off this ride."

"Ready," he said. "Let's do it." He stood up and tucked Blight the purple hippo into his front pocket. She spared one brief thought for the rose she'd shoved down the side of her bra, since she had no pocket option. Sometimes the damn retro look which gave her an excuse to wear gloves was a giant pain.

Metal *screamed*, drowning out the sirens. The Ferris wheel lurched to the side and Michaela tumbled back in the seat, accidentally pulling Bane with her. This time, it didn't feel like it was going to stop.

Chapter Eight

"LET'S GO!" HIRO SHOUTED. How could Michaela still be *easing* his panic? Without her, he'd still be stuck at the very top of the Ferris Wheel, curled into a little ball and drowning under the weight of his fear. She lifted her hands off of his arm, taking her tranquil energy with her. Fear immediately flooded back in, closing his throat and making his breath come in pants.

He'd never met a superhero empowered to manipulate emotions. In fact, he'd never known that type of power *existed*. The scientific part of him wanted to sit Michaela down and ask her every tiny detail. Did it only work through her hands, or would any skin-to-skin contact do it? Was it purely mental, and temporary? Did her power affect hormones, or neural pathways, or the actual structure of the brain in a permanent way or...*Not the time, Hiro. Examine all the aspects of this discovery later. Don't die, now.*

He took a deep gulp of salty air and looked over the railing. *Oh, so far. So far down.* In real height they were probably three meters above the pier, but in acrophobia height they were stranded on an insane cliff overlooking a hellish abyss.

The Ferris wheel slumped further to the side. Metal beams *screeched* as they bent, piercing his eardrums.

"Alright. Let's try," he shouted.

She gave his fingers a reassuring squeeze and nodded. He accepted the burst of calm she'd sent in that touch with gratitude. They moved side by side, climbing over the edge. Combined, their weight made the bucket creak and tip. Gripping the safety bar with all his might, Hiro looked at Michaela and swallowed. "Ready?"

She nodded at him.

"Go."

They let go at the same time and tumbled into the bucket seat below. The impact made it swing wildly. Hiro's stomach rolled like the waves under the pier.

Slowly, torturously, the Ferris wheel groaned as it leaned even further. It could be minutes until the supports snapped. Or maybe only seconds.

Again they swung their legs over the edge and clung. "Look down," Michaela told him. "Short drop now. It's going to be fine."

He risked a quick peek and saw she was right. "Yes." Seriously, how was she so calm about all of this? "Okay. Go!"

Never, in his whole life, had he been happier to feel the brutal impact of a hard landing. Together they sprinted for safety, ducking under shredded awnings, dodging crushed games. It would have been suitably theatrical for Hiro to hear the booming and cracking of the Ferris Wheel falling behind them as they ran. But real life lacked a sense of drama and they had reached the parking lot on shore before the wheel snapped, fell, sliced through the railings, and skidded into the sea.

Hiro gathered Michaela into his arms for a tight hug. After basically surviving his worst nightmare the relief was too huge for a friendly handshake. He ached to hold on to her.

She folded against his chest but kept her hands flat at her sides, palms pressed to her thighs. Someone or something must have given her a strong impression that her power was a bad thing. She'd kept it a secret until necessity forced her to act. She wouldn't touch him now the danger had passed.

But now, Hiro had the answer to why he'd felt something strange in the urgent care with her. The problem he'd been working over in his mind for days had been solved. He knew one of her secrets. Triumph rocketed through him.

He rubbed a hand lightly against her back and she snuggled closer. Her white rose, slightly crushed, stuck out the bodice of her dress still valiantly lit with rainbows. He smoothed his hand across her shoulder, trailing down her arm. When he slipped his hand under hers, she stiffened and tugged it away.

"Bane," she said warningly. "It's not a good idea, to t-touch my bare hand."

He grinned. "I think it is. I like touching you."

"But it's—I can't. I'm not supposed to. Never."

Lacing his fingers through hers again, he lifted her hand to press a kiss to the back. A riot of emotions pulsed from her and straight into his heart. He trailed tiny kissed up her arm and tried to sort them out. Fear stood out the clearest...probably she didn't want her secret exposed. A pang of her regret slipped through. A deep, resigned sort of sadness underlaid everything else. Nervous anticipation, a timid hope. And a tiny hint of arousal as his lips touched her bare shoulder.

"Only you get to say what you're supposed to or not supposed to do," he told her quietly. "Don't worry about supposed to. What do you *want* to do?"

Finally, she smiled. "I want to be able to hold your hand." Despite the small curve of her lips, her emotions pulsed with pained wistfulness. As if she'd never been able to simply hold someone's hand. It seemed unspeakably sad to him.

He squeezed her fingers. "Then do. I like it. I'm glad you were here, Michaela." He hoped she could sense how much he meant that.

"You wouldn't even have been on the damn Ferris Wheel if not for me."

"But I wouldn't have lived through it without you. What you can do is pretty amazing."

"You're not so bad, yourself." She glanced around, as if to make sure everyone was still too busy rushing about to overhear, then leaned closer. "Are you sure you don't want to be a superhero instead? You were pretty heroic today." Softly, she disengaged their fingers and hid her hand behind her back.

"Be a superhero? And ruin a nice day for everyone by fighting right through a crowded carnival? Nope, thanks. I'm happy on the other side. I hadn't heard Sea Bitch planned a battle today. I'd have tried to warn you if I'd known." As he could have guessed, the combatants had already disappeared beneath the water again. Taking their battle with them and leaving destruction behind.

Like always.

She leaned back and searched his face. "Do you hear about every battle? Beforehand? Is that a supervillain club thing?"

Although he'd been considering taking her hand back, he was glad now that she'd pulled away. He didn't want to hurt her with these particular emotions. Bitterness seethed through him so strongly he was afraid it might etch into her soft skin. "It's my thing. I like to know what's going on. But I don't hear about every battle."

Michaela sighed. "Well, aside from almost getting killed, I had a really good time today, Bane. Thanks for everything."

She smiled once, quickly, and turned to go.

He let her make it a few steps. "That sounded a lot like a brush-off." He darted in front of her so she had to stop. "'I had a really good time, thanks,' is always code for a 'but' coming up next."

Staring at his chest, she shrugged. "Of course it's not. I just, you know, I figured you wouldn't be interested. In seeing me again." Her gaze scooted to meet his, then retreated back to his chest. "After someone finds out about what I can do, they usually don't want to be around me anymore."

"They're afraid," he guessed. Those tiny pricks of feeling attacked his heart like an asteroid shower now, gouging, digging in, making room. Pretty girls who could be ruthless were alluring enough, but pretty, ruthless girls with tragic secrets *really* did it for him. "They don't like knowing you can dig around in their personal head space whenever you want."

Her shoulders hunched protectively, and she cupped her elbows. "It's not whenever, it's only when I touch someone. With bare hands." With each word, her voice lowered until she was whispering. "And they always hate it. Always."

Deliberately, he reached out to pry her hands away from her arms. She pulled away, eyes wide, but he held on. He gave her hands a gentle squeeze. "I'm not afraid. And I don't hate it."

"You will." Her expression stilled with absolute certainty.

Through their linked fingers, sadness vibrated through her and straight into him. It was a wide, cold, lonely world of sad and it was intimately familiar to him. His chest ached.

She pulled her hands from his grasp. "Bye, Bane. I had such a good time today."

"I will be calling you," he told her.

She shook her head as she walked away.

Chapter Nine

MICHAELA KNEW SHE WAS being stupid. She knew she should have expected it. She'd told him exactly what would happen, in the parking lot at the end of their perilous first date. A word for word prediction of the future.

After people find out about what I can do they usually don't want to be around me anymore. Her warning had been sincere, based off of demonstrable fact.

But...*I will be calling you* he'd said. Like he didn't care about her power. As if he'd be different from everyone else. She knew better than to trust it. But her silly, soft heart had somehow believed him anyway. She'd set herself up for the blow when he didn't send more than one measly text.

Super busy just now, call you later?

Almost seven days, seven whole words, a couple texted memes, and zero calls. Give it up already, Michaela.

Her day had been long and exhausting at urgent care. Case after case, the less serious injuries from yet another super battle which had impacted the freeway in the early hours this morning. Sprains, strains, tweaked backs, lacerations, bruises. One dislocated shoulder. A broken collarbone.

The worst cases had gone straight to the emergency room, but she'd heard through rumors that it wasn't as packed as normal after a big combat. Captain Champion generally kept his conflicts short, sweet, and civilian free. Most of the time, Michaela appreciated his unusual consideration. But today it meant the patients ended up in urgent care. Therefore, a non-stop, no-time-for-meals, barely-time-to-pee day for Michaela.

Part of her started to think Bane was really onto something. It had never bothered her this much. Not consciously, anyway. Maybe deep down she thought both supervillains *and* superheroes could choose their battleground with a little more care...but she'd never thought she'd say it out loud. Huge, destructive, raging encounters were a part of life. People lost cars, houses, buildings, even their lives, every day.

Villains tried to take over, and the superheroes stopped them. That was the way the world worked, the way it had *always* worked, and she'd never questioned things before.

She would never be one of the strange fanatic group who wanted all Empowered to go somewhere else, preferably another dimension, and let the Unpowered live with no interference, no powers. The MundanƐ wanted no Legion watching over them. No protection. Everyone—apart from a zealot—knew supervillains hurt whoever they could, powers or not, and supervillains had superpowers. Superheroes and sidekicks were the only way to stand against them.

She knew how the world worked and that universal constant was part of the reason she'd gotten her LPN after she left the Legion. As a nurse, she would always be needed and she loved knowing she made an actual, tangible, helpful difference in people's lives.

But the danger The Sea Bitch and Water Wonder had put them in had infuriated Bane. She'd *felt* his rage when he realized they would have to fight for their lives simply because they'd chosen to go to a carnival on a Monday afternoon.

She rolled her head to the side, stretching to release some of the tension tightening her shoulders. Before she could stop herself, her eyes zipped over to examine the bush Bane had hidden behind last Sunday. No figure hiding there today, of course. She cursed at herself under her breath. Why was she still looking?

Six days. Aside from one sparse text, she hadn't heard from him in six entire days. Tomorrow it would be a week since their disastrous first date.

She was an *idiot* to be surprised. Only one person in her entire life had ever accepted her power and that person wasn't The Evil Bane.

She unlocked her car with an angry twist of her key, fell into the driver's seat, and slammed the door. But instead of starting the engine, her traitorous hand picked up her phone. Her heart sat up and begged her to hit the *call* button under his contact information. Or to text him.

But it didn't matter what her heart wanted. This was real life and in this reality, her powers scared people.

Really, she should be grateful to him. Her heartache would be so much bigger if she'd let herself get attached. If he'd spent more dates pretending he liked to hold her hand, her emotions would overwhelm him. Eventually it would get to be too much, like it did for everyone else who knew what she could do. It was better he'd found out before she could really get involved.

Still, she wished...if only Sea Bitch and Water Wonder hadn't picked *that* particular day. The exact, specific pier in Ocean City with a carnival. She'd been having so much fun. And their kiss still burned, seared into her brain. Then she'd had to use her power and it ruined everything, like always.

Sighing, she tapped her head against the hard plastic of the steering wheel. *Quit it. Just stop, Michaela. Let it go. You had one really fun date and that's all you get.*

She started the engine. Time to get home to her apartment and delete some of the useless numbers in her phone.

· · · ·

MICHAELA YANKED THE wheel to the side, ignoring annoyed honks from behind her, and threaded the car into the parkade. She dug into her purse with her free hand, trying to get to the ringing phone. Her heart thumped and her fingers shook as she pulled it out.

The screen informed her, in pitiless color, that the photo popping up wasn't who she'd been hoping to see.

She inhaled through her nose, let the air out, and put on a smile. Then hit the green *answer* button. "Hi, Furia."

Smoothly, she pulled into her assigned parking space in front of the apartment building. She turned off the car and tipped her head against the headrest.

"Michaela." Furia's tone was neutral. Usually a bad sign. "How are you?"

Drained? Heart-sick? Fairly sure I'll die alone and only my plants will notice when I stop watering them?

"Great," Michaela said. "Fine. A bit tired. It was kind of a long day today, what with all the injuries."

"Injuries? You're injured?"

"Nope. I'm fine. The battle this morning? On the Freeway?" Michaela hinted. "Colossive was being transported from one ultra-max to another and Dead Loch tried to break him out? I heard something about you and UberMeta Man and a task force with Captain Champion."

"Oh. That's right. I'd forgotten. They're both being transported to Winter Max facility as we speak. There will be no more trouble from those two."

"Right. Yes. But there were many civilians injured in the battle, Furia. A lot of them ended up in urgent care—where I work." Even approaching the *edge* of sarcastic like this was far out of Michaela's normal scope when talking to Furia and she couldn't suppress the instinctive wince.

But she shouldn't have worried. She could practically *hear* Furia shrugging over the phone. "There will forever be evil in this world. And good will always rise up against it."

"Uh-huh." A newly awakened part of her wanted to *scream* until Furia finally understood just how bad this attitude was. Michaela frowned. "Is UberMeta Man still in town?" Hope fluttered, but she'd learned not to count on it.

"No, he's on a mission. He's in demand a lot right now." Furia sounded apologetic. "I'll ask him to stop by soon."

There was always a mission. Mentally, Michaela waved her tiny hope goodbye. "Was there anything specific you wanted today? I just got home and I'm headed in."

Enticing thoughts of a nice, big, frosty cup of water finally drew her out of the car. Water, and a pair of aspirin for the naggy headache tightening the back of her neck. She absentmindedly tucked the phone between her ear and shoulder as she strode towards her building.

"Yes. Michaela, I'd like you to come to dinner with me tomorrow. Our Monday evening dinner. It's been weeks since you and I had time for it. And there's someone I'd really like you to meet."

Michaela stopped cold, right in front of the double Titanglass entry doors. She spared one brain cell for the person who thudded into her back after the unexpected halt. Hopefully, whoever it was would walk around her to get where they were going, because she stood frozen in horror.

Inside the lobby, separated by titanium-threaded glass, she could see Mrs. Fish waving in her direction. She smiled weakly back at her beloved neighbor. "Someone you'd like me to meet? Is this another blind date? Are you setting me up again?" Her headache ratcheted up another degree, radiating down the nape of her neck.

"Of course not! This is simply a meeting between friends. And I'm sure you'd like to meet Scott. He is a *catch*. Steady, reliable, hardworking, polite, a great conversationalist."

So, basically a really well trained terrier. Michaela rolled her eyes as she pushed open the door. The person she'd just brake-checked crowded in behind her. She'd have to apologize after this torture disguised as a phone call ended. "A steady, hardworking catch. Who's polite. And single?"

"Well, yes. He's a doctor, Michaela, just starting his residency at Smallcity Health."

"Mmm."

"He'll be joining us for dinner with Sharon. You remember Sharon?"

"Mm-hmm," she said. "Look, Furia, I appreciate the thought but I just can't. I don't want to be set up. With anyone. At all." The last two words were almost a whisper. Her stomach lurched shakily. She still wasn't used to saying no—especially to Furia.

"I know you don't, which is why this is not a set up. Just a dinner between friends."

Michaela barely stifled her groan. Mrs. Fish waved again, her giant canvas shopping bag slung over her other arm. *Coming*, she mouthed silently at her. *I'm coming.* For some reason, Mrs. Fish kept waving, even more enthusiastically.

"I really do appreciate it, Furia, but I don't think—"

"It's been such a long time since I saw you last, Michaela. I'd like to see you. Come to dinner."

Great. The guilt tactic. Her resolve, weak to start with, crumbled. "I—alright. Dinner. Tomorrow." A tiny bit of assertiveness flashed its fin above the prevailing tide of defeat. "But it is *not* a date, and this Doctor Scott had better not think it is."

"Of course not. I'll see you tomorrow evening. Seven O'clock, at *Il Finocchio*."

"Seven, *Il Finocchio*." Michaela repeated wearily.

"And, Michaela?"

"Yes?"

Furia hesitated for a beat. "While we're at dinner, it's fine if you go ahead and refer to me as *Mom*." A tiny laugh vibrated through the phone. "I'll have the restaurant well-cleared of any villains by the time you arrive. And Sharon already knows who you are. It will be safe."

"What? I mean, sure. In front of Sharon, *and* this Scott? Um. Of course." Michaela came to a halt in front of her neighbor, who had finally stopped waving. Now, she was grinning. "Well, goodbye. See you tomorrow, Mo-Furia." She couldn't quite unstick the word *mom* from her throat, even with implicit permission.

She sagged forward and leaned her forehead on Mrs. Fish's shoulder. As always, she carried the comforting smell of oranges and the cinnamon gum she was never without. And as always, she supported Michaela without question.

Mrs. Fish patted Michaela's head gently. "Aren't you just the best-looking thing I've ever seen walk in here?"

Michaela snorted. "I feel like road-kill that got dragged in, but thanks. I'm so glad to be home. What a fucking day."

"Didn't mean you," her neighbor said cheerfully.

Her voice was projecting, over Michaela's head. To the person behind them. The mystery person Michaela had road-blocked, who had most likely followed her in here for an apology. *Dammit, dammit, fuck, I hate today.* She considered just keeping her head on Mrs. Fish's sturdy shoulder and refusing to acknowledge them.

A smooth, familiar voice smashed into her chest like a blow. "We need to work on your ability to tell people '*no.*' And by people, I mean everyone but me. Obviously."

Michaela whirled so fast her braid whipped around and stung her on the mouth. "*Bane*? What are you—"

Standing in the middle of her apartment lobby, smiling sheepishly, he looked like the best thing she'd seen this whole miserable day. And he hadn't called. He'd snagged her heart with hooks made of sunshine and fun and a rainbow rose, and then ripped them all out when he let her walk away.

Then the idiot tracked her to her apartment building just in time to overhear her talking, awkwardly, with her own mother. As if she needed *more* reasons to feel vulnerable around him.

"NO," she snarled at him, and darted behind Mrs. Fish.

Chapter Ten

HIRO HELD HIS SMILE hard in place. He shifted his secret weapon further to the side, keeping it hidden until the opportune moment. She was absolutely as upset as she had a right to be. *Should have called, dude. Found a spare second, somewhere, and left at least a message. Shit.*

His mind reeled after the revelation he thought he'd just overheard. The Fabulous Furia *had* to be more than Michaela's superhero mentor. It was his job to hear everything, but he'd never heard of Furia being particularly close to anyone. Definitely not close enough for regular Monday night dinners.

He'd also never known anything like Michaela's power.

How many more secrets lay buried inside her? What other surprises did she have in store for him? And how much did he want to discover them?

He eyed the lady Michaela had hidden behind, weighing up his chances.

She crossed her arms as she stared sharply back at him, one elegant eyebrow arched. The woman's skin was several shades darker than Michaela's. Her salt-and-pepper hair swept up and back into an intricate knot. And her outfit shouted *casual classy* in each flowing line of fabric. As defensive walls went, she was a damn good one.

If he wanted to get the girl, he'd have to go through this powerhouse of a woman. Empowered status and opinion of him, unknown. Options, getting slimmer by the second. Risk, high.

Hiro warmed his smile a few degrees. "Hello, I'm Ivan. Ivan O'Reilly. I'm here to see Michaela."

Michaela's barrier snorted at him. "You're good looking and smooth talking. I'll give you that, *Bane*." She emphasized the name Michaela had called him by, ignoring the civilian cover he'd tried to use. "But my Michaela obviously doesn't want to see you. I ought to just stick a fork in your balls and let you know, you're done."

He couldn't help the instinctive wince and crouch, almost dropping the bakery box. No one wearing testicles could hear that phrase and stay upright.

"I want to see her. Please? I need to apologize," he said, gripping the box and forcing himself to stand tall again.

Silence. A transport of some kind zoomed above the street, blaring bass thumps which reverberated off the door frame behind him.

"Apologize?" Michaela asked. She peeked out from behind the other woman. "Are you going to say you had a good reason for leaving me hanging for a week?"

Hiro winced again. "I didn't actually realize how long it had been until I looked at my phone this morning. And then I knew you were at work, so...Hi. I'm here now."

"You were that busy?" Michaela's guardian managed to pack a lot of disbelief into one sentence.

"Look, I brought food," Hiro said desperately. He held up the bakery box he'd been hiding and waved it, temptingly.

Michaela peered over her friend's shoulder and narrowed her eyes at it. "Oh, well, buttercream definitely soothes the sting of rejection," she said. "Let me just forgive you right now."

She might be angry, but she still let her sense of humor out to play. Hiro thought he might have a small chance. "I didn't actually say cake was involved."

"It had better be," the other lady put in, primly. She stepped a bit to the side, leaving Michaela exposed. Unspoken permission for him to go ahead and try to work things out.

"It's cupcakes, actually. Lots of buttercream. And lemon, um, cream?" What had the lady at the bakery called it? Curd? Curd sounded like what happened to your food *after* you ate it, not what you wanted to eat. "Maybe some...fondant? I don't really know much about cake." He couldn't believe how much he wanted to step over there and get Michaela in his arms. Somehow, everything in the room looked brighter around her cheerful yellow scrubs. How had five—okay, six—days evaded him so fast?

Michaela pressed her lips together into a thin line and glanced up at her friend. When the older woman nodded, her stance relaxed slightly. "Bane, this is my neighbor. Mrs. Fish, this is The Evil Bane," she said.

The woman nodded at him and put a hand on Michaela's shoulder. She might have stepped aside for the moment, but she was still firmly on Michaela's team. "A supervillain? That's going to be interesting, honey. And my name is Nadine, but you'll call me Mrs. Fish like everyone else," she said to Hiro.

"It might not be interesting. It might not be anything. We'll see how this apology goes," Michaela said.

He stepped closer and held out the little white box of goodies for her to appraise. "Just a chance to explain. That's all I'm asking." His eyes needed a good splash of ice-cold water. They felt sandy and full of grit. The few hours of sleep he'd snatched this afternoon hadn't been enough.

She took her treats from him, careful to avoid his fingers despite having on the blue plastic-y gloves he recognized from her work. "I can give you that. Hold on, one second. Were you waiting because you need something Mrs. Fish?"

Mrs. Fish shook her head. "Not a thing. You go on up. I'm glad I got to meet you, Bane. Apologize right, or I'll know. Michaela won't have to tell me a thing. I'll know anyway. And I got no problem throwing you out."

He grinned at her. "I like knowing where I stand. I'll apologize perfectly." He reached over to the box in Michaela's hands, nudged it open, and took out a yellow-frosted cupcake for Mrs. Fish, which he presented to her with a little bow.

The older lady chuckled and accepted it. She didn't make it a point to avoid brushing against his fingers, and yet somehow never actually touched his skin, either. Interesting.

Then she held out her free hand, palm facing up, to Michaela. Michaela stripped off a glove and laid her own palm flat against it. Like a children's game on the playground, played so often it had become a solemn rite.

Hiro's eyebrows shot up. Michaela hid her power from the world and refused to touch anybody with a bare hand. Except when it came to her neighbor. Her protective, affectionate neighbor, who stood in front of her and covered for her without thinking twice. She might not have mentioned a *mom* in any context, but it seemed *Mrs. Fish* fulfilled the meaning of the word just fine.

He could sense the edges of something...something big and comforting and real moving between them in the time between one heartbeat and the next. So strong he could nearly *see* it like a heat shimmer in the air. Michaela took her hand away and the sensation vanished. Mrs. Fish waved and turned toward the door leading outside.

Without looking his direction, Michaela headed for the stairs. Clearly, whatever strange ritual she had with her neighbor was not up for discussion.

"No elevator?" he asked.

"It's getting repaired. Or retrofitted. Or something."

"Ah." He should have remembered but there were so many repairs to keep track of. That's what he hired contractors for. "Which floor is yours?"

"Fourth. I'm four-oh-five."

"Okay." He followed her up and up. Every time his hand reached forward to grasp hers, he eyed the stiff set of her back and thought better of it.

They reached a plain wooden door with brassy gold numbers, 405. Michaela's hands quivered as she unlocked it.

Hiro had been entertaining thoughts of a vague apology with much emphasis on the 'let's move forward from here' bits. They were gone now. He knew Michaela's power, and where she lived. A suspicion about who her mother might be tingled at the back of his mind. He'd met Mrs. Fish and seen how important she was to Michaela.

She didn't even know his real name.

There was a major imbalance between them—one he needed to fix. The only way forward was honesty. He'd give her as much as he possibly could.

Chapter Eleven

MICHAELA TOOK HER TIME setting her cupcakes on the kitchen counter. "Look around, if you want," she told Bane. "Um. The bathroom is down the hallway there." She gestured toward it, keeping her back to him.

"No, I'm good. But thanks," he said.

Michaela shrugged. In a world where supervillains guarded the location of their lair viciously and superheroes kept hideouts deep inside unreachable mountains, visiting someone's private space could be taken as an indicator of trust. Part of her trusted Bane enough to let him inside her apartment...which was too much to think about right now, so she focused on getting herself some water.

Her favorite part about being granted the privilege of visiting someone new was seeing how they'd chosen to arrange their space. She *loved* comparing decorating, judging people's house plant choices, and getting new ideas. But she didn't hear Bane moving. No footsteps, no rustles as he walked around her tiny living room, no whisper of paper as he spied through her bookshelf. A supervillain should at least snoop a little.

By the time she had her big glass of water and a smaller one for him, all of the air seemed to be slowly leaking from the room.

He stood in the middle of the carpet, right where she'd left him. Somehow he dominated the average sized room, becoming the focal point. The man wore nothing but charcoal gray shirts with dark pants, and for some reason this lack of fashion sense made her all gooey inside. Something was officially wrong with her.

She wanted to open the door, shove him out, and shrink the room back to normal. Or walk over there, press him to the wall, and bury herself in him until all of the oxygen disappeared and both of them were gasping for breath. Even odds, either way.

Instead of doing either of those things, she sat at the edge of her couch. With a hand wave, she indicated he could sit, too. He perched at the other edge and accepted the glass of water she handed him. If she'd been able to forget the pinpricks still poked through her heart and climb on his lap, skip right past this uncomfortable conversation, she might have. Physically, she had no issues with him.

"So. Apology?" She gripped her condensation-slippery glass between both hands and stared at his shoes. Black shoes. Of course.

He shifted a few inches closer. "Do you remember, at the pier, when you asked if it was a villain thing to know about battles?"

Thoughtfully, she lifted her eyes all the way to his knees. "Yes. You said it was your thing, that you like to know what's going on."

"That's it. I didn't finish that sentence for you then. The rest of it goes—*so I can warn everyone in the danger zone to get out.*"

"What?"

"I try to stay on top of upcoming battles so I can help evacuate the people who will get hurt."

He made no sense. Supervillains didn't do things like that. And it didn't explain why he'd been too busy to call. "You, what, call people at home like a...telemarketer. And tell them to get out? And they listen to The Evil Bane?"

His mouth quirked. "No, of course they wouldn't listen to me. But Ivan O'Reilly is a part-time reporter who works for Smallcity Broadcasting. He emails the local safety and fire departments, and *they* call people. They've learned to trust him over the years. His information is always good. The Chief of Community Safety is positive Ivan O'Reilly is a hacker, by the way, but he chooses to let it go."

She met his eyes and scooted close enough for their knees to touch. "You do all of that? Seriously? Ivan O'Reilly is the silliest cover name ever, by the way." Sitting this close to him, she could see what she'd missed in the apartment lobby. Exhaustion, pulling down the muscles in his face and slumping his shoulders. A ring of irritated red surrounded his dark eyes. Even his sexy-Bane grin looked tired.

He laughed quietly. "I know it. That's why I chose it. And yes, Seriously. I do have to hack into a lot of things. It's lucky my power is with technology and sensing how it works. Besides the potenkinesis, that's my power, I mean" He floated his water glass over to the coffee table as a reminder. It settled onto the wood with a tiny *click*.

Then he held his hand out to her, palm up, waiting. His eyebrow arched, making his expression a challenge. Michaela's heart hitched. She could hardly believe it...he would let her sense the truth, or lack of it, behind his words. He would willingly put her inside his defenses, even after he'd experienced what she could do. No one had *ever* trusted her like this.

She took another sip of water, stalling, and set her cup next to his, eyeing his outstretched hand warily. Then she reached out. Her fingertip brushed his warm, flat palm and she absorbed the jolts of emotion. *He really is sorry. Determined. Focused. Helping people is...so important to him. He means every word.* She pulled her hand back, breathing through the squeezing in her chest.

His palm dropped to his knee.

"Keep going," she said, circling a finger to indicate he continue. "That's amazing, and really heroic of you, but it doesn't explain why you disappeared for days."

"I'm so sorry. I'm sorry I let the time eat me up without calling you. I just get hyperfocused and forget to stop." He sighed. "Okay, at first I was giving it the required two days so I didn't look pathetically eager, even though I was. But after that, I got too involved to think straight."

She couldn't keep her mouth from going a bit crooked. No one knew more than her about the type of person who got too focused to remember anything else. No matter how important. Like stopping for meals. Or picking up their daughter from school—regular civilian public school, of course, because a simple control over emotions wasn't big-time enough to rate sending your daughter to Riverdale Powers Preparatory with the other superpowered kids.

"So. I find out about battles and I try to get the civilians evacuated," he summarized.

She nodded.

"Okay. It's really cool how easily you believe me, by the way." His dimple flashed and nearly blinded her. "That shows trust, which is important to any relationship."

"We don't have a relationship," she said, but she let her smile go from crooked to straight.

"We're going to." He sounded so determined. "Also, when I find out about the battles, I...change the situation, when I can."

"Change the situation. Like where the battle are? To save more people?"

"Whatever will work. It doesn't always. This time I had to hack into the Ocean Max system. The incapacitated idiots had the transfer for Colossive scheduled for 5:30 yesterday evening, if you can believe it." He rolled his eyes expressively.

She shifted a little closer, until their legs pressed together. "For the middle of rush hour, on a crowded freeway, through the closest major town, *knowing* someone would be incredibly likely to try breaking Colossive out. In other words."

"Exactly. I tried requesting through safety department channels that Ocean Max change their schedule, that took most of Wednesday. But Ocean Max wasted a ton of time demanding to know how the department knew anything about their secure plans." He waved this useless concern for security away with an impatient gesture that amused her.

"There was a ton of back and forth and accusations and the poor Chief couldn't exactly admit he uses hacked information. So I did a little more digging. I created a few bugs. That took me most of Friday and Saturday." He closed his eyes and tipped his head back. "Like, ah, random locking and unlocking sequences for the doors to the weapons room. And turning off all power in the motor bay. I might have also set their sound system to a disco channel and possibly tripped the shark alarm when there weren't actually any sharks. Kind of." Bane blinked, giving her a sleepy version of his usual smile.

Imagining the chaos, Michaela started giggling.

"By the time they got everything sorted, and the guards back from turning off alarms, and got the trucks running, it was after midnight last night. So they had to do the transfer much, much later than they had planned."

"And the battle happened at three in the morning and hardly anyone was on the freeway!" Michaela finished for him. "Everyone wondered why they'd picked such a low traffic time. The ER couldn't believe it. We were so busy at urgent care."

"But no serious injuries?" he asked, sitting straight again.

"Almost none. I did hear two of the guards from the Ocean Max truck were in critical condition."

He grimaced and scrubbed a hand over his face. "I tried."

Michaela noted the bruised-looking circles under his eyes again. "You worked for two days straight on hacking into a high-security super max prison system?"

"A day and a half. The rest of the time was creating the bugs. Fortunately, I'm really, really good at that and I have a bunch ready to go whenever I need them. I only have to tweak the code to fit the particular system I'm trying to sneak them in to."

Michaela gave up.

Letting new *Brave Michaela* take over, she climbed into his lap to sit facing him. The way she'd been wanting to since he sat down on her couch. She linked her hands behind his neck, keeping her bare skin away from his skin. Her headache was forgotten, the long day and fraught phone call rapidly fading into the background.

He pursed his lips. "I seem to be forgiven."

Michaela held up her index finger. "*If* you can promise to at least explain a bit more in your text the next time. A couple memes, hilarious as they were, will not do it. You need to try. It's not okay to disappear for days at a time. Not so good for you, either. You need to sleep and eat. Especially to heal that arm."

"I slept. A few hours here and there. Right now I'm feeling pretty energetic. And I promise to do better next time." He brushed a kiss against the edge of her lips. "I promise."

She leaned into the gentle touch. "You're forgiven."

"Just like that," he sighed against her lips. "You're wonderful. Did you know that?"

"What you did...what you do. It helps a lot of people."

He gave her another kiss, light and teasing against the other side of her mouth.

"It did hurt," she told him. "Thinking you'd ditched me. I thought you'd decided I was right and my power was too much for you. But I understand getting too focused to stop. I understand saving people."

"I won't do it again. I don't like hurting you." He lowered his forehead to rest against hers and squeezed her tight against him. She let herself melt, heat to heat, pressing against his hard chest. He murmured, "I'm just...not used to checking in with anyone. You'll have to remind me."

Although she wasn't touching him with her bare hands, a flicker of loneliness puffed from him to her through the air as a tiny, icy-blue cloud. Then it was gone.

He feathered light kisses to her cheekbones, down her jaw. Then he swept his tongue across the seam of her lips. Her heart stuttered, misfired, then started again, revving up to twice the usual speed. He used his hands to trace her shape as they kissed, squeezing and smoothing at hips, waist, ribs...until she was caught in a web of tingly, hot need.

When the tips of his thumbs brushed underneath her breasts she whimpered. Tension coiled in her, so tight and achingly sweet.

"I don't know how I could have been dumb enough to miss out on this," he said with a groan.

She nibbled on the taut cord tracing up from the hollow of his throat. "You were busy saving Smallcity." With her forearms she traced the shape of his shoulders, finding the hard muscles underneath his shirt.

Finally—finally, his hands shifted to tease her nipples through her scrubs. She arched against his touch. "Tell me why you're a supervillain again?" she asked.

He swept over her breasts with his thumbs, torturing her through the barrier of her shirt and thin bra. "Because I do bad things to superheroes."

"Mmmm. Right," she said. At the moment she couldn't care less what he did to superheroes. They could take care of themselves. "If you could just do some bad things," she undulated her hips, pressing harder against the bulge she could feel in his jeans, "yeah, right here." He abandoned her aching nipples to grip her hips and roll her against him. She breathed in his ear, "Yes, please."

His laugh puffed against her neck, sounding strained with desire.

Chapter Twelve

HIRO TRIED, AGAIN, to gulp in enough air to calm his overheated body. Extra oxygen failed spectacularly to calm anything at all. A sudden bucket of ice water might not even be enough when Michaela took away everything else in the universe.

With her sweet weight pressing him into the couch he barely noticed there *was* furniture. He didn't see the room around them. Hear the people or traffic outside. His self-control disappeared. His exhaustion faded. She was the sum of his world right now, each piece and particle of him attuned to her.

He worked his way up her neck to her jaw with tiny kisses, breathing in the sweet-tart lemony fragrance that was so very Michaela. When he reached her mouth—that lush, perfect mouth—he couldn't fight the need to devour her. And didn't want to. She met him, matched him, until they were sharing the same breath.

She still hadn't touched him with her bare hands.

She held him carefully, caressed him with her forearms, rubbed her knuckles over his shirt down the line of his spine. But she wouldn't contact his skin with her bare palm.

He couldn't blame her for being afraid. After she'd told him that everyone else ran away from her unusual ability, he had pretty much disappeared. In her mind, it must have confirmed everything she'd said. She hadn't known about Hiro's obsessive, workaholic savior complex. It would take time and more than a bare apology to make her feel safe enough to share it with him again. He could wait.

Whether she meant it or not, he took her refusal to touch him as a clear signal. She needed to grow her confidence, more than a few days to trust him with her secrets. He wouldn't touch her hands. Not until she let him know it was something she wanted.

Hiro needed some time too. She wasn't the only one with secrets, and he didn't want to spill them all tonight by brushing against her hand on the couch. Worryingly, a little part of him already wanted to throw everything out there. To say *actually, The Evil Bane isn't my true name*, and give her his real one. He'd never felt that urge with anyone else and the strength of it frightened him.

Could a supervillain *really* confide the deepest, most damaging parts of himself to The Amiable Accomplice?

Panting, he broke their kiss and leaned back. She looked dazed, pupils so wide her eyes were black, reflective pools. His erection strained against the zipper of his pants hard enough to ache.

"Dinner." He forced the word out on a puff of air.

"What?" She softly kissed the side of his mouth, then his chin...his resolution to slow down a bit nearly broke.

"Food. You need some. I need some. Let's have dinner."

"You want me to cook for you?"

He rested his forehead against hers, clawing back some control. "Are you a good cook?"

"These are the important questions." She nodded. "Yes, actually. I am."

"Perfect. I knew you were perfection the first time I saw you." He smoothed his hands along the slight curve of her back. "I actually wanted to order something and feed you. Kind of a date. It's been a long day for both of us, I know I'm exhausted, and I thought we could use a break. What do you say?"

She grinned. "I say, tacos."

"See? You're flawless." He let his hands wander down to her ass, so he could cup her curves and torture himself a little more. She squirmed on his lap, exponentially increasing the delicious distress.

He swallowed back a groan. "Just looking for your phone," he told her. "Mine's in my back pocket and I'm sitting on it."

"I'm in scrubs," she pointed out, both breathless and teasing. "Which have useless little back pockets."

"So?" He squeezed her ass again. "I'm just checking. It's got to be here somewhere."

"So my phone isn't back there." She snickered. "Side pocket."

"Right." He caressed his way down her thigh and reached inside her pocket. He drew out a pen, a roll of white medical tape, small silver scissors, a triangular plastic cap with nothing attached to it, lip balm, and a fuzzy mint.

She burst out laughing.

He couldn't help but join in. Still giggling, she leaned far enough away to dig into the pocket on the front of her shirt.

"How many *side pockets* do you have on there?" he asked.

"Lots. The back pockets are completely worthless but there are two front ones here," she pointed to her pants, "one down the side here," she pointed at her left leg, "and two here." She gestured to the front of her bright, sunshine-yellow shirt.

"Order what you want but give me the phone when it's time to pay," he said.

"Thank you. And you can stay here to get some sleep after dinner if you want. I don't—oh yikes, that was not a euphemism for anything." A deep rose flush started to creep over her cheeks. "I meant literal sleep. It was a long day. I think we both need some rest. And...I'm not in the right space to want sex right now. I'm still absorbing your explanation, but I don't want to waste any more time without seeing you, either."

Hiro hadn't even considered going from full stop to immediate start after he'd been such an ass. He brushed his fingertips over the alluring sweep of color on her cheekbones and made an affirmative noise. "I'd like that. Thank you."

A night of snuggling sounded amazing after he'd missed an entire week with her. But cuddling could lead to talking and Hiro was already concerned about how much he might say. She wormed her way right inside his walls without even trying, spun herself into the center of his universe just by being there. He had to wrestle with the insane urge to tell her his name, his thoughts, his plans, *everything*. Everything he'd never told another person.

She was more dangerous to him than a multitude of superheroes. And he didn't even care.

Chapter Thirteen

MICHAELA WASN'T PRECISELY looking forward to her dinner with Furia. She flattened the side of her hair, making sure the pins holding it back were still in place. The effort was wasted since she couldn't really feel them through her black silk gloves. But her hair seemed to be staying, mostly, so that was nice.

She shifted her fingers down to tweak the embroidery dancing along the neckline of her dress and pick at an imaginary loose thread. Stalling...but she couldn't quite get her mind and feet to agree on walking inside the restaurant just yet.

Somehow, she'd never connected with her own mother. She had no idea what she'd been doing wrong her whole life, or how to do it right. They just...had nothing cohesive to bind them together. Both of them wanted a loving relationship. She had *felt* the wistful ache for it from Furia. And her mother did try. She'd made sure Michaela was combat trained by the best and attempted to force the entire Smallcity Legion Chapter to accept her as a sidekick. Through sheer strength of personality, and the Fabulous Furia had a *lot* of personality, so a sidekick Michaela had become.

But Michaela hadn't inherited either parent's power, or even the same level of power. She'd barely made it into the Legion, squeaking through when UberMeta Man had backed her mother up and made it explicitly clear he would like to hear plenty of *ayes*.

He was the most powerful superhero for several galaxies, invincible, unmovable, and he'd made no secret of the fact that he wanted to see more heroes with a variety of powers in the Legion of Superheroes. From the day he'd smashed his way into Riverdale Powers Preparatory as a teenager and insisted on staying, he'd made equal treatment his agenda. The part Michaela loved most about him was that he was simply too powerful for anyone to throw him back out. He'd made her dream, openly fighting on the side of good, possible.

But even with UberMeta Man's support, Michaela knew most of the Legion saw her as a token low-powered member. There only to fill UberMeta Man's quota and not on the merit of her own skills. She'd worked her *ass* off to train, fought in so many battles she'd nearly failed high school from constant truancy...and she was still looked down on. It had been a major factor in her decision to leave the fighting and pursue a career in nursing.

And her mother would never forgive her for that decision. Michaela didn't particularly want forgiveness for doing the right thing. It created a barrier between them neither seemed to know how to cross.

Michaela smoothed a hand down the skirt of her cherry-red dress again, then sighed. *Il Finocchio* looked the same as always, floodlights outlining the building against the deep blue of a summer evening sky. Rich scents mixed deliciously in the air, roasting peppers and sharp tomatoes, spices, cheese, and a sweet undertone of coffee.

Dinner would be wonderful. The company, not so much, but she could get through it. She always did.

Her mother stood at the edge of the parking lot, off to the side of the crowded entrance, partially behind a decorative shrub. Avoiding attention, a habit for every superhero. She wore a black dress as unlike her flame-colored super suit as night from day. It snugged over her short, curvy body like a stylish glove. Her rich, deep auburn hair glowed in the lights from the restaurant.

Michaela raised a hand to acknowledge her mother's wave and headed towards her, heels click-clacking on the asphalt. She scanned the shadows next to Furia, preparing herself to meet well-housebroken doctor Scott.

But instead of the formal suit jacket she'd been dreading, next to Furia stood a tall man wrapped in a shimmery royal blue super suit. . .

Michaela broke into a run.

She slammed into him and wrapped him in a hug. "UberMeta Man! I didn't know–"

Strong arms enveloped her. The stretchy, scaly material of his suit scratched against her cheek. "I can't stay," he rumbled. "But I wanted to stop by and see you two on the way to the Legion hall. It's been too long."

She buried her face against his broad chest, squeezing him tight, and inhaled the sharp scent that belonged only to her father. Something like acrid gunpowder, a bit like the tang of distant stars.

His gentle touch against her back reminded her they were in public. She stepped back while all three of them reflexively looked at the crowd. Someone was always watching; the question was whether or not that someone was a minion. If a supervillain found out that UberMeta Man appeared happy to see this particular civilian...

"I checked when I got here," Furia said with a smile for both of them. "Still, it's good to look again. How have you been, darling?"

He seemed a bit tired, but as unbreakable as ever. People in three galaxies knew his distinctive blue and gold suit on sight. Affectionately, they called him *The Man of Titansteel*. Michaela was proud to have his thick black hair and identical large, dark eyes. She liked to think she'd gotten the best of both parents in looks, if not with her powers.

"I'm fine. Good. Same as always," he said. "Flying around, saving worlds. I was in Jotunheim last week, that was fun." He shrugged. "There are many calls."

Michaela nodded. He loved her and Furia and she'd never doubted it, but he was UberMeta Man. "I heard about the convoy attack a few days ago. It sounded like a big one."

His brow wrinkled for a moment. Then he appeared to remember which battle she was referencing. Deep lines etched around his eyes and mouth, making him appear stern despite his rare smiles. "Oh, the convoy. I remember. There's been a lot of other places since." He waved all of them away with a dismissive gesture. "And how have you been, Michaela?"

This evening contained a zero percent chance she'd be reckless enough to mention she'd started dating a supervillain. "Great," she said. "Mostly working. Lots of work."

"Just work?" he asked.

"Pretty much. I did make it out last weekend to get some sun and air in Ocean City."

"Good. You've always loved the beach. I'm glad..." he trailed off to cock his head sideways. His wide shoulders slumped a micro fraction. "I'm so sorry, loves."

Michaela pressed her lips together, forcing her instinctive protest back down her throat.

Furia moved to his side to give his arm a brief caress. "You heard a call?"

He nodded and a kissed her temple. "Always," he murmured into her hair. He stepped away. "You look beautiful, firebug." Stretching out an arm, he gestured to Michaela to come in for a hug. "You both look so pretty. Enjoy your dinner, sweetest-heart."

She treasured the old, familiar nickname as much as the solid press of his arm across her shoulders. With another kiss for her mother, he was gone. He lifted into the air over the parking lot, moving so fast she blinked and missed the moment he disappeared.

She and Furia stood together on the asphalt, shifting awkwardly. A fire truck sped through the intersection, lights and sirens going full blast. As the wails died to echoes, Michaela voiced the question she'd kept inside her entire life. "Does he always have to go? I mean, every time? Couldn't someone else do it once in a while?"

It was a Bane sort of question. Without trying, she'd even used his inflection.

Furia eyed her in disbelief. "Yes, of course he does. UberMeta Man is *always* needed."

"Right." Michaela sighed. "He is."

Michaela could feel her mother's gaze burning into her as they walked, searching. She'd never once, in all these years, hinted that she resented the constant calls which kept her father away. Furia couldn't comprehend the idea of questioning it. When Evil threatened, heroes rose up against it.

Furia's entire life was built around this unchangeable fact and there was no room for anything else inside her.

"Speaking of need, have you considered what I said, about coming back to the Legion?" Furia asked. "You're still a sidekick. You're still a valuable part of our side."

And here came the opening shot of the evening. Michaela couldn't even work up a wince. She'd known it would be coming. *I-Messages*, she remembered. *Stay away from accusing You-messages.* "I feel like we've already covered my reasons for leaving plenty of times," she tried.

"I just don't see how a few insensitive comments could be *that* terrible, Michaela, and we really could use your help–"

No, Furia just didn't *want* to see the daily realities Michaela faced. It was too difficult, and uncomfortable for her mother. "The word we talked about was *microaggressions*, mom, and there were plenty. Remember how many people assumed I couldn't hold my own in a fight and tried to keep me 'safe'? Or super-splain every step to me? Or—my favorite, asked me to fetch them drinks during a meeting?"

"Sexism is something every superpowered woman has to face. I've had to my entire life. We face it, and we overcome it, like every other evil."

Michaela held up a warning hand, amazed at her own bravery. She'd *never* tried to push back on her mother's self-centered views like this before. "Let's just leave it alone, okay? We don't see things from the same position. And I'm ready to eat. Not argue."

At her side, Furia shrugged. But she looked a little stunned by Michaela's audacity.

After they entered the ornate front doors, Furia scanned the crowd. Her mouth twisted sideways in an impatient scowl. "I don't know where Scott has gotten to. But there's Sharon. She's waiting at our table." She waved to the woman sitting alone at a table for four.

Michaela smiled. Maybe this Scott had been held up. He might not even make it. He was probably equally unenthusiastic about this set-up and trying to avoid it without making it obvious. Furia's temper flared in a quick, hot echo of her power and intimidated many people.

A touch more confidence propelled Michaela to their table. She could handle dinner with her mother and Sharon Jameson.

Sharon, her mother's best friend, rose to give Michaela a brief hug. She was a sub-editor for Smallcity Broadcasting. Almost thirty years ago, still a lowly freelance reporter, she'd discovered Furia's secret identity while investigating a story. Rather than capitalize on the knowledge she'd become a family friend. Michaela had never asked how that worked. She was officious, nosy, a status snob, relentless in her pursuit of a lead, but also unquestionably loyal.

She stood to greet them with brief hugs. "So good to see you." She beamed at both of them as she took her seat again. The short, asymmetric cut of her blonde hair swung perfectly into place above her ears.

"I'm starving." Furia reached for her menu. "I don't think we'll wait for Scott. He's obviously been held up, but he hasn't bothered to call."

Michaela hid her tiny smile behind her menu. It took a strong person to stiffen their scrotum enough to call her mother and back out of an invitation.

"That nice doctor you told me about?" Sharon asked. Her tone implied she had a scoop on Scott's absence.

Michaela pretended to study the entrée choices.

"He left a message with the hostess. She caught me on the way in. His car broke down, right in the driveway. It wouldn't even start, he said. It's actually lucky." Sharon paused, as Michaela could have guessed she would. Having a juicy new tidbit to share was the reporter's favorite thing and the delivery could not be rushed.

Furia knew how to play along. "Lucky? Really. How so?"

A waitress approached to get their drink orders. Michaela asked for peach iced tea and settled back for the show.

"Because I have a replacement." Sharon let a few more beats of silence pass, building up the drama, taking the time to place her napkin just-so on her lap. Her huge, sparkly rings glinted on her fingers, even in the dim candlelight of the room. "One of our best young journalists. He emailed me asking if I knew any ladies who might be interested in meeting him. He said he trusts my judgement more than anyone else in the department. And when I asked, he said he's ready to settle down." She winked at Furia.

The waitress returned with their beverages. Michaela thanked her as she set down the iced tea. Her hope started to deflate, seeping away like sunbeams on a stormy day. Reprieved from the master villain only to be shoved right on the train tracks.

She cleared her throat and took a sip of her iced tea. *Say something! Say you don't want to be set up with anyone. Not now, not ever again!* The words wouldn't climb out of her head to land on her tongue. Her new assertiveness had disappeared somewhere.

Furia sat up straighter. "Is he any good? Is he dependable?"

Sharon leaned across the table. "I've only met him a few times. He works freelance, from home. But–" she lowered her voice so Furia and Michaela had to press forward to hear, "–he is absolutely reliable. Although he keeps his sources a secret. He always seems to be right on scene when there's a battle between Empowered. It's like he knows when they're going to happen." She raised both eyebrows.

Michaela's hand jerked, accidentally pushing her fork into her salad plate so that it gave an embarrassing, loud *ting!* Something about this sounded so familiar.

Sharon slid her gaze to Michaela and smiled, inviting her into the secrets she was dishing out. "He's only twenty-eight and he's gorgeous, Michaela. Dark hair, piercing black eyes. I believe his family is from Japan, although I've never asked. So I can't swear to it."

"He sounds interesting," Furia admitted. "But freelancing. From home. Does that make for a good income?"

Sharon moved her hand in a sideways *so-so* gesture and took a sip of her lemon water. "It doesn't always, but in his case it's absolutely a steady income. He is such a good investigator. He'll always have work. Don't worry about that." She leaned back, settling into her chair, and casually dropped her bomb. "I called to invite him after the hostess made it clear Scott wouldn't be able to come. He'll be here any moment."

Furia twisted to scan the restaurant. As though this mysterious, dark, and handsome journalist would pop out from behind the nearest potted fern. "Sharon! I haven't been able to investigate him," she hissed.

"I have, and I've known of him at SCB for years. Trust me, my friend."

"Well, what's his name?"

Michaela had a definite feeling about the immediate future. She could have mouthed the name along with Sharon. A kaleidoscope of butterflies took off whirling in her stomach and she clenched her hands tightly in her lap to hide their trembling.

"Ivan," Sharon said. "Ivan O'Reilly."

How the *hell* had Bane managed it?

Chapter Fourteen

HIRO KEPT HIS SHOULDERS back and his chin raised as the hostess showed him to the table. He had the same feeling he always got just before a battle. Anticipation, focus, the rush of adrenalin. His fingertips tingled, and he had to make an effort not to fling handfuls of nanobots out of his pocket to set up a perimeter.

Not a battle, he reminded himself. *No combat. Down, boy. You're just meeting Michaela's mom. The superhero. And you're a supervillain. And all of us are in our secret identities in the middle of a crowded restaurant. What could go wrong?* Even inside his head the sarcasm sounded clear as a bell.

The tableau of expressions before him made him *wish* he'd worked a camera into his suit jacket.

Sharon—poor unsuspecting coworker—looked like she'd singlehandedly negotiated a cease-fire between the Capulet and Montague superfamilies.

The Fabulous Furia lowered her brows, hazel eyes fiercely drilling into him as he approached. It had been a gamble, whether or not she would recognize him in civilian clothes, but he wore that obnoxiously distracting face mask as his Bane costume for exactly this reason.

His chest constricted at the sight of Michaela, as if he hadn't left her all tousled and glowing after his kisses at breakfast this morning. She'd done something soft with her hair, pulling the sides back and leaving the rest tumbled, highlighting her dark eyes with shimmery gold. And her dress made her look like the most delectable present he'd ever ached to unwrap. Of course, she had the same effect on him in sweats and a ratty sleep shirt, with bedhead.

Keeping his hands off of her was going to be such a struggle, he decided not to bother. He'd just have to be sneaky about it.

Act one, scene one. Hiro widened his smile. *And, action!* "Hello," he said as he approached the table. "I have to apologize for being so late. I hope you didn't wait for me too long."

"No, no, not at all!" Sharon trilled. She stood up to shake his hand. Her grip latched on like a pincer. "I'm so glad you could make it on such short notice." She tugged him to the side of the table where Furia sat.

Furia stood slowly. By her side, Michaela also rose. Seeing them together, without the distraction of a super suit or a fight getting in the way, the resemblance was clear. Michaela had her mother's fine cheekbones, the same pointed chin. They had a similar height, and stance. Only her coloring was different, a deeper olive tone to her skin along with her black hair and eyes.

"Ivan, this is my good friend Fae Martin and her daughter, Michaela. Fae, this is Ivan, our intrepid reporter from Smallcity Broadcasting." A touch of anxiety threaded through Sharon's tone. He was here to meet Michaela as a possible date, but they all knew which introduction was most important.

Before Furia could react, Hiro lifted her hand to touch a light, polite kiss to the back of it. The old-school move would throw her off balance. "Charmed. So nice to meet you, Fae." He smiled. "That dress is stunning. You look very fierce."

"It's nice to meet you, Ivan." Furia's gaze devoured his face as she tucked her hands behind her back. Without a trace of embarrassment she scanned him from suit collar to shoes, looking for something. Probably hints of weakness. Evidence of depravity. Anything that didn't look good enough for her daughter. She'd eat him alive and toss the raggedy remains out the restaurant door if he let her.

He deliberately turned his back to her and greeted Michaela as if she were a stranger. "This must be the lady I've heard so much about."

Smile growing, she moved closer. "And you're the Ivan O'Reilly *I've* heard so many good things about."

Hiro reached for Michaela's hand.

Sharon's hand covered her mouth, failing to hide her horror. He heard Furia's footstep behind him and rejoiced in the conundrum he'd caught her in. Michaela had gloves on, but they couldn't be *sure,* could they.

Michaela stared over his shoulder, her expression tense. If he had to wager, he'd put everything on the theory that Furia was giving her a look designed to forbid her from shaking his outstretched hand.

What's it going to be, beautiful? Are we defying the Fabulous Furia together? He stopped with mere centimeters to go, leaving the last move up to her. She could turn her hand over and take his offered grip—or back out of it.

Not only did she take his hand, *she took her glove off* before their hands met. "It's nice to meet you," she said softly.

He gave her a much less polite kiss than he'd given Furia and both her tiny sense of triumph and his own wave of pride in her twirled through him. Mixed in were her amusement, her disbelief, determination, and a slight touch of fear. "*Such* a pleasure to finally be introduced, lovely Michaela," he said.

They looked at each other over their linked hands. Hiro's heart gave a victorious leap. For one endless moment, no one else in the restaurant existed.

Then Furia nudged him. Not gently. "Why don't we all sit down, now that we're introduced?" A punch of heat needled into his side and he grunted. Her smile was bright, if a touch feral.

Another pulse of anxiety came from Michaela.

He squeezed her fingers before he let her go, trying to send her some reassurance. "Why don't we? I've heard wonderful things about the food here, but I've never tried it before."

"Yes," Sharon said breathlessly. "It's delicious. We—we haven't ordered yet." She sat, shoulders relaxing. "We waited for you."

"Thank you," he told her. He took the empty chair next to Michaela and nudged it closer, so their thighs touched under the tablecloth.

Michaela shot a sideways look at him and cleared her throat. An adorable blush started to rise above the neck of her dress.

He opened his menu, made a good impression of someone actually reading it, and enjoyed the warmth of her body next to his.

Sharon and Furia watched them intently, ignoring their menus, with nearly identical expressions on their faces. They might as well have held up score cards with, *she's never taken her gloves off for a stranger before! 0/5 stars* printed on them. He would bet his entire lair and a least two of his companies that they were trying to decide if that show of boldness from Michaela was an indication they should start considering wedding colors...or march his ass out of the restaurant right now.

The waiter gave him a brief reprieve by coming over to take their orders, forcing them to take their eyes off him at least a little.

Once he'd left, Furia pinned all of her attention to Hiro again. "So, Ivan." She sipped her drink. "Sharon tells me you're a reporter and you specialize in supervillain battles. That seems dangerous."

He shrugged. "Not as much as you might think. A lot of my work is done online. Everything is all about computers, these days."

Her gaze sharpened. "You hack into their systems?"

All the time. "Of course not. That would be illegal. And immoral." He focused on smoothing his napkin in his lap, hiding his expression. Furia put clues together quickly and accurately. "I find sources and I use them. A lot is easily available in the public domain if you know what to look for. Company records, fees, permits, pay scales, licenses. I'm more an unanticipated, unpaid secretary than anything."

"Speaking of companies. Some of us at SCB think it's time to investigate E.B. Industries to see what it might be hiding," Sharon said. "It's such a huge, public company. There's no way it's not a cover for *something.*"

Hiro barked out a laugh. "If there was ever a shield company for an alter-ego, I can assure you E.B. Industries is not it. It's the silliest name I've ever heard, for one thing. Sounds like a company that produces bumblebee themed toys."

Sharon and Michaela barely reacted to his weak joke. Furia scowled.

"That might be your next assignment but I just can't believe you'll find anything," Michaela said earnestly. "E.B. Industries owns my apartment complex. They're the one paying for all the safety upgrades in the building and they haven't even raised our rent to cover it."

"They sound almost too good to be true." Hiro let sarcasm exsanguinate freely into his tone and rubbed her calf with his foot. She rolled her eyes at him, and her lips twitched.

"Their focus on safety is a little overdone," Furia said. "Smallcity is kept safe by its superheroes. There's no need for these reinforced walls and highway barriers and—and shatter-proof Titanglass. I think your investigation should start with their source for all of these high-tech innovations. *Someone* had to create what E.B. sells."

This was getting too far into dangerous territory. And distracting him from feeling up Michaela. Time to go on offense.

"I already had a new article in mind, actually." He turned to Sharon. "Let me know what you think. A piece on the unpowered casualties caused by superhero battles, something focused on the total damage. The property losses, the injuries, and the amount of work this gives the local hospitals. I'm willing to bet over half of their patients come in as a result of Empowered battles."

Furia straightened up so fast it seemed like an electrified wire had popped out of her chair and stuck her. She gave him a burning glare. "I doubt that. That seems like a bit much. Superheroes do everything they can to save lives!"

"And yet, so many lives are lost daily," Hiro said coldly. He let his foot slide up Michaela's leg again, well aware of the challenge he had just thrown down in front of one of the fieriest superheroes in the entire city.

Between Furia's enraged expression—clearly stating that she'd love nothing better than to lunge across the table and burn his trachea out—and Michaela's thigh resting against his, he'd never enjoyed a dinner more.

Chapter Fifteen

WOULD SHE *ever* be able to look her mother calmly in the eye and deliver that kind of zinger? Michaela sincerely doubted it. She'd used every ounce of available bravery tonight just to remove her gloves.

She slid her hand beneath the tablecloth to shove Bane's leg again. He didn't budge, flashing a quick, sideways grin at her.

If she had any courage left, she would brush her fingers on the bare skin of his wrist, forcing him to feel her shock, awe, amused exasperation, and her disbelief at his nerve. She couldn't, of course. No one wanted her feelings pushed at them constantly.

"I'd be interested to see your *facts* and figures after you're done with this new article," Furia said. Her voice dripped acidic disdain.

The air surrounding Bane burned against Michaela like a fever and she knew it was her mother's power. Touching Bane's bare hand had been a bad enough start. Discussing the damage caused by superheroes only made Furia angrier because she refused to acknowledge it ever happened.

Michaela took a deep breath, trying to lay calm like a blanket over the tension coiling deep inside. Soon she'd start stuttering and fighting the urge to leave, and for once in her life she wanted to stay. To stick this uncomfortable conversation out. To make her own opinion heard.

And Bane was here with her. That made all the difference.

Sharon sat silently across the table, toying with her silverware. Poor thing. The cuddly kitten she thought she'd invited turned out to be a tiger, and she was going to hear about it from Furia later.

"Facts. Of course," Bane said.

To Michaela's absolute shock he started to trace patterns over the back of her hand, tickling, sending tingles up her arm. He...*wanted* to touch her. The way she hadn't dared touch him. The contact gifted her with his emotions; a calm sort of amusement, a touch of smugness, excitement, and a fierce desire to connect. *With her.*

Her eyes stung. She turned her hand over to grip his.

"I'm all about the fact gathering," Bane said, leveling Furia with an intense gaze. "I think I'll start by interviewing some of the insurance adjusters in Small City. See where it goes from there. And I'll even let you see my article before anything is published."

Michaela slid a quick glance at him. He sounded so civilized but his expression blazed with fierce challenge. She'd never seen anyone other than her father hold Furia's eyes for so long. Not without turning into a walking fireball, anyway. A cold spike of real fear lanced through her.

Bane flinched and let his gaze drop back to the table.

"Yes. You do that. I would like to see it before your editor rejects it," Furia said.

He kept his face tilted down but Michaela felt his reassurance. His feelings as good as told her *don't be afraid, I've got this.*

Internally, she scoffed at him. *Don't try that on me.* If she had actual telepathy he could hear her, instead of guessing at hieroglyphic feelings. *You have no idea what Furia might do to you.*

Their waiter appeared with their food and started setting plates on the table. "Oh, look, my salad!" Sharon said, a little too brightly. Michaela had never heard anyone sound so happy to see wilted greens.

Her fingers shook as she picked up her fork. She forced herself to grip tighter and stabbed blindly at her plate. "You m-might not know this, Ivan, but I work at a local urgent care facility. I'm a nurse. I...might be able to help you gather facts."

She took a bite of cucumber that she didn't taste and refused to turn her head to see her mother's reaction. Bane's face lit up and she bathed in its glow.

"I *didn't* know that," he said, the innocence in his voice a tad overdone. He chewed his salad, looking thoughtful. "You could be a huge help to me. Privacy laws are so complex. I need some major assistance finding out what I'm allowed to access, for a start."

His free hand slipped under the tablecloth again. He patted her knee, almost comfortingly, but then his hand crept up. And up. And *up*. "Perhaps I could get your number. We could meet up to work on it some time."

Michaela jolted so hard her fork dropped to the table. His warm touch burned through the thin satin of her dress, all the way up her thigh. So distracting. She poked him with her forefinger, pushing down, but it was the opposite of helpful. The skin-to-skin contact only added the heat of his arousal to hers. Still, he did retreat to her knee. She inhaled slowly.

"No," Furia said.

Michaela choked on her breath.

She and Bane looked to Furia at the same time. But under the table, he twitched her skirt aside, sneaking beneath her dress to touch her bare knee. Her heart thumped against her ribs. Tension and excitement battled through her until she was afraid she might shatter into pieces. This was so not the time, and yet it was the best time.

"No?" he asked Furia, sounding distracted. "I'm afraid I'm not sure which part your 'no' refers to."

He ran his fingers up the sensitive skin of Michaela's inner thigh, scorching her. Branding them together as they secretly, shamelessly contradicted any *no*. When she was with her Evil Bane, consequences didn't exist.

But playing under the table was pretty daring, even for a sidekick brave enough to date a supervillain. Why wasn't she making him quit? Was she actually turned on by getting felt up in a restaurant?

He reached the edge of her panty line and traced a finger along it, causing her tickling, tingling torture. The muscles in her stomach contracted. Her nipples tightened, pushing deliciously against her bra. Yes. Yes, it was turning her on.

"No. You may not have my daughter's phone number. And no, she will not be helping you write this baseless smear piece." Furia lifted her head proudly. The glossy red mass of her hair flowed over the straight line of her shoulders. "She knows as well as I do that superheroes do nothing but good for Smallcity. You should think about keeping the focus of your article on the evil deeds of supervillains. The focus of *all* your future articles."

He sat calmly in the face of all Furia's heat, while his warm hand traced her pussy over the silky material of her panties. Michaela fought to control her breathing, to give nothing away. She shifted her hand from her lap to cover Bane's thigh and smoothed her way up.

"The editor decides what gets published, Fae. You know that," Sharon soothed. "And he'll never let a slander piece into the paper. I think there's something important in finding out more about E.B Industries and their inventors. There must be an entire team working behind the scenes to come up with all the things they've been selling! Imagine finding out the names of the people giving us so much security. People would *love* that. They'd be so grateful."

For some reason, this made Bane's grin broaden. Michaela squirmed in her chair. Did he already know what was going on? Had he hacked into E.B. Industries? Shivers danced up and down her overheated skin. She bit back a gasp when his finger pushed at the top of her slit, seeking out her clitoris. Oh, Powers, her panties weren't enough of a barrier when she was this wet.

"Yes. That would be a much better idea for an article." Furia picked at her salad, separating out the onions with a grimace. "An article like that should keep you busy, Ivan. Much too busy for dates."

Her sideways glare at Bane made it clear. He was gone after she allowed him this one, failed dinner.

And he was fingering her daughter's clit through her panties, right now.

Michaela clutched her fork with one hand, although she'd long since stopped pretending to take any bites of food. With the other, she traced the outline of the bulge in Bane's pants. She flattened her palm against it, rubbing. Smooth material, rigid male inside of it.

Bane's finger froze. He cleared his throat.

Like everything else about her supervillain, this was more enjoyable than she would have guessed. Naughty, wicked, fun. In the last few days she'd started to figure out how exciting it could be to let go and misbehave a little.

Okay, a lot.

She pressed harder, discovering his long, hard length, the flared crown at the top. Smiling slightly, Michaela released her useless silverware to take a leisurely sip of her tea and explored Bane's cock under the table. His zipper got in the way a little. Touching him without really being able to *feel* him only made her hungrier.

She'd never expected to enjoy tonight's dinner this much.

"Busy," he agreed with Furia, his voice slightly hoarse. "Ah...a piece like that would, definitely keep me very busy. But I could still make time for a social life. I'm afraid you aren't in control of who does or doesn't get Michaela's phone number." His fingers shifted, continuing to tease Michaela through damp material.

She trembled. *No one* defied Furia like this. And here she was, firmly on Bane's side against her mother while they did super inappropriate things under the table. A part of Michaela she'd never suspected was coming out to play.

Furia stared at him, open scorn plain in her twisted lip and her raised chin. "I'm her mother. Of course I have a say in who Michaela spends time with. You obviously lack focus, intelligence, and integrity. I don't consider you a good date for my daughter."

Sharon's eyes narrowed, gaze flicking to the edge of the tablecloth. *Oh, no.* If she started thinking up reasons for Michaela's flushed cheeks and Bane's throaty voice... If she thought to check, all powerless hell would break loose.

Regretfully, she drew her hand away from Bane and patted his thigh. *Later*, she promised them both. *I'm going to see, touch, and taste every inch of that. But later.*

He shifted his hand, squeezing her thigh gently before he settled the hem of her dress back down to its perfectly proper length below her knee. Her whole body throbbed and ached with pure need.

She turned her head to flash him a sultry smile. This was easier when she wasn't actually looking at Furia. "I think you make a great date. Let me get you my phone number."

"Why thank you. Yes, please."

"No," Furia barked. The fork in her hand started to glow red, the salad dressing clinging to it sizzled. "Absolutely not."

Chapter Sixteen

HIRO KEPT QUIET, EVEN as heat pulsed over him in frenzied waves. He defied superheroes every day. It was a routine part of the job and one he enjoyed. Someone had to knock their arrogance down a peg, or sixteen.

But this was Michaela's mother. And Michaela was obviously used to folding under Furia's wishes. How far they'd take their defiance tonight was up to her. He'd back her up even if it came to a superbattle through the middle of this restaurant.

...Although leaping dramatically from his chair would be harder than usual with this erection stretching against his dress slacks. He'd figure it out. Whatever Michaela needed.

Michaela kept her head level, her eyes steady. "Actually, Mom, I'll keep seeing Ivan if I want to." Hiro winced at the strain in her voice.

"He has completely the wrong idea about superheroes, Michaela. He might even sympathize with supervillains! He could be a *minion*, for all we know." Furia spat the word with as much disgust as she would saying *murderer*.

"He makes some good points. The battles *do* hurt people," Michaela said softly, shifting her gaze to her silverware.

"How can you say that?" Furia looked stunned.

"Because it's true. I treat the injuries every single day at work." Her entire body trembled, but she bravely kept going. "And I will date him if I want to. It's my choice. Mine." Still pressed against his, her leg stiffened and tensed.

He gripped her shoulder and squeezed comfortingly.

A searing flash of heat from Furia burned a red smear across the back of his hand and crisped the leaves of the decorative plant behind his chair.

He hissed out a curse and jerked his hand to his chest, honestly shocked. Was the superhero angry enough to risk *revealing her identity*

84

to an entire restaurant full of civilians? Did she regularly forget herself so badly? Michaela sure hadn't inherited that reckless streak.

Or—had she somehow guessed his identity and decided to treat him like the supervillain he was?

Hiro wanted to put his arm around Michaela, even if Furia decided to burn it harder. His hand throbbed, but he was still half aroused, tensed for imminent battle, and he couldn't have been prouder. A spine of plasteel ran through this beautiful, compassionate woman. He knew it. She just needed a little nudge to grab hold and stand with it.

Those little slivers of emotion he had worried over at the pier had set up a nice big home inside his heart, growing, expanding, changing everything. It was terrifying. It was exhilarating.

He dipped his napkin into his glass of ice-water and spread it across his burn.

"You will not give him your phone number! Or see him again. I forbid it," Furia snapped at her daughter.

Michaela must have caught his movement, or heard his cursing. Her hand shot out to catch his wrist and she gasped. Her eyes flew to Furia's. "How could you do that?"

Hiro was overwhelmed by her shocked fury, and the wrenching, tearing effort it was costing her to fight like this.

"He shouldn't have his hands on you." Furia's tone was devoid of any repentance. "You just met. What would your *father* think of him and his wild ideas?" She put a strange emphasis on the word.

"Fae..." Sharon didn't appear to be able to think of what to say. Her eyes were wide with dismay as she watched the drama play out in front of her.

Michaela let go of his wrist and leapt from her chair, sending it flying behind her to smack into the wall. "I don't care. I don't care what either of you think. I'm old enough to make my own choices. If my choice is him, you have *nothing* to do with it. You don't get to pick. Not anymore." She chopped apart air with her hand, a savage negation.

Hiro got to his feet beside her.

"Where are you going?" Furia demanded.

"To find a bandage to cover this burn." Michaela indicated his hand with a jerky nod. "Thanks for dinner."

"No, Michaela, don't. Don't go. I only want what's best for you. I want you to be safe. You know that."

"I do know that." Michaela's tone made it clear what she thought about her mom's definition of safe. She shook her head and turned to him. "Are you ready to leave?"

"Of course." Hiro brushed a hand against her cheek. The thin skin on the back of his hand gave a raw twinge. A sad smile tilted her lips, and it was worth it.

He turned to Sharon and offered her a nod. "Thank you for inviting me. It's been the most interesting meal I can remember."

She let out a weak sound which might have been acknowledgement, or even agreement.

With her arms wrapped around herself, Michaela walked away from the table. Hiro dug his wallet out of his back pocket and scanned the bills inside. He pulled out what he figured was sufficient and dropped the pile at his empty place. "This ought to be enough for your dinner. Please, enjoy it," he told the two ladies.

Furia looked after her daughter, completely ignoring the money. "Don't leave with him," she called, less fiery than before, more desperate. "I don't want you to have anything to do with him. Do not make me go after him. Don't force me to call your father."

Hiro caught up to Michaela just as she turned her head to look at her mother. "I've been old enough to pick my own dates for years," she said quietly. "Go ahead. Call Dad. And, and never set me up on a blind date again. I *hate* them."

Hiro took Michaela's hand and they walked out of the front door of the restaurant together.

Chapter Seventeen

MICHAELA WASN'T SURE where to go after her intense exit from *Il Finocchio*. Movies made this kind of spectacle look easy. The heroine would deliver some kind of fantastic line—the kind Michaela could only think of three days later in the shower—and then fly dramatically to the front door, hair and cape flowing behind. She'd probably take a cab, which *of course* would be waiting right outside. The cab would drive under the kaleidoscope lights of the city, accompanied by poignant background music.

Background music sounded great. All Michaela had was an achy chest and a strong urge to scream. And no theme song. What she'd said was true—asserting her wishes like an adult, yeah, about time. Long past time, actually. So...why did it tear a raw wound inside her to do it? Shouldn't she feel powerful, or vindicated? Or at least happy?

Bane stood next to her on the sidewalk with his arm around her. He didn't say anything, just held her. Soft summer night flowed around them like warm ink. Cars sped past on the wide main street. The Riverwalk streamed on the opposite side, a bright daisy chain of lights. People brushed by them to enter the restaurant. Ordinary sounds, city sounds, blended into a burring background.

For one moment she rested her head against his shoulder. Let herself sink into his wordless support. But he was hurt, and she couldn't relax until she'd treated his burn, so she started automatically for the closest first-aid kit she knew of.

As she guided Bane towards her car she couldn't quit scanning the night sky, looking for the flashing shadow which meant UberMeta Man. Her mother would call on him. It was only a matter of when.

Bent over the first aid kit spread out on the passenger seat, Michaela tipped her head enough to get a look at his jawline, a hint of his expression. "Bane?"

"Yeah?"

"Thanks.

His profile shifted as he smiled. "I enjoyed that."

He probably had. Fighting superheroes was a daily thing for The Evil Bane. But it was far, *far* out of the normal scope of The Amiable Accomplice.

In fact, The Amiable Accomplice had never felt so sick to her stomach.

She dragged her fingers through her supplies in one frustrated swipe. "I don't have any gauze pads. Damn it. I haven't replaced the last ones I used yet." Frowning, she shifted a bundle of band-aids back into place. "I should start keeping burn ointment in my kit, too."

"You would have a first aid kit in your car." He sounded amused.

"Well I can't treat your hand with what's here. Let's go back to my apartment. And we didn't get our dinner. We can hit a drive-through on the way for burgers. Do you want to come with me, or follow in your car?"

He shook his head. "I walked, so I'll come with you. Burgers sound fantastic. And...you've got another first aid kit in your house?"

After tucking her small med pack under the passenger seat, she indicated for him to sit. "Um, yes. A good one with everything I need. Doesn't anyone take those public announcements about battle and disaster kits seriously?" She eyed the dark sky again.

A gentle kiss pressed against the top of her head, distracting her. "Oh, my sweet summer child, no one even *watches* those."

She snorted.

While they settled into her car she asked, "What did you do to Scott?"

Bane laughed out loud. "Me? Do something to whom? Why would The Evil Bane concern himself with one civilian doctor?"

"Bane." Her lips twitched. She maneuvered the car around and shifted into drive.

"Fine. Fine. I didn't do a single thing to poor Scott."

Michaela focused on merging into traffic, waiting.

"I did it to his car."

"You broke his car?"

"Of course not! That would be a crude solution. I am pure finesse."
He sounded genuinely offended, but when they flashed through the
spot of light under a streetlamp she caught his unrepentant smirk.

"Right. Sorry. Pure finesse. So, what did you politely do to his car?"

"Removed a spark plug. I even brought him a new one to replace it.
I set the box safely to the side. It had a shiny bow on it." He sounded
aggrieved at the thoughtlessness of people who couldn't find the
gift-wrapped replacement for their own stolen car parts. "I guess he
didn't find it in time to pop it in and get to the restaurant. It's just
as well." From her peripheral vision she caught him shaking his head
woefully. "Dinner might have gotten a little awkward."

She'd never heard such an understatement in her life. "I'm not even
going to ask how you found out his full name, car type, and address in
less than twenty-four hours."

"Best not to."

"Bane," she sighed. "You're terrible."

"Yes, hello? Hi. Supervillain," he reminded her.

• • • •

INSIDE HER APARTMENT Michaela finished the last wrap of
medical tape and nipped off the end. "There. Just keep it dry for a
day or two. It's only a first degree burn, it should start scabbing over
soon. We'll put some antiseptic ointment on it if it starts drying out too
much."

"I love it when you talk all medical to me," Bane said. "Do it again."

She laughed. "How's your pain level? Do you want some
acetaminophen?"

He rested his forehead against hers, and their breath mingled.
Michaela closed her eyes and enjoyed the warmth.

"No," he said. "I don't need any."

She cracked one eye open and pursed her lips at him. "Bane. Don't be brave for no reason."

He smiled, his eyes still closed. Those sculpted, kissable lips curved and her gaze caught on them. "I'm not. I'm a huge baby about pain. Remember? It's really not that bad. Just aches a little."

"Tell me if you change your mind. I'm sure your arm isn't all the way back to normal yet, either. My poor Bane."

"Hmm," he said, a noncommittal sound that could mean *yes* or *no* or *it's healed* or anything.

Michaela wrapped her arms around him and crossed her wrists behind his neck. She'd left her gloves piled on the seat of her car, and the guilty urge to dig another pair out of the giant collection in her closet faded every second she spent pressed against him.

If she could, she'd instantly fix every wound on his body. She'd tell him how amazing he'd been in the restaurant. How completely different from her normal timid self she'd been, knowing he was there to back her up. She'd confess how much of her heart he already owned.

That huge of an admission was too scary right now, but she could easily admit how much she wanted to run her hands over the lean strength pressed against her.

"Michaela," he murmured. "I've got to kiss you. And I'm fairly sure we won't stop there, but I know tonight's been hard on you. Just tell me if I you don't want sexy times right now."

"I want sexy times," she told him. "I want all of it."

He answered with a kiss. The need in it was raw, immediate. She was lost before she knew it, arousal ramping up with stunning speed. It *had* been a hard dinner. Right now, she only wanted to forget all about it.

She pulled back only to change the angle and take the kiss deeper. He buried his hand in her hair, used it to grip and tug her where he wanted her. Pins landed softly on the couch and tendrils of hair brushed her cheeks. She didn't care. Behind his back, her hands curled into tight fists.

The need, the craving for him slammed through her like a wave—over her head, drowning her. "Touch me," she panted, and leaned into the brush of Bane's fingers along the sweetheart neckline of her dress.

He took her earlobe between his teeth, nipping gently. Her stomach clenched sweetly. "Just, be careful of your hand," she reminded them both.

She tugged at his suit jacket, pulling it down his arms. The lamps in her tiny living room highlighted his deep gray shirt, the hint of shine in the material. Michaela ran her eyes over it appreciatively. "That's a nice shirt. You look great in it, but we should definitely take it off. Wouldn't want to get it dirty."

He grinned. "No, we wouldn't. We should get this dress somewhere safe, too. It's so pretty. Did I tell you how beautiful you look tonight?"

Her heart stuttered. "Yes."

"Oh. Well, I'll do it again. You're exquisite," he said and slid a soft kiss along her collarbone.

Her fingers shook as she unfastened the buttons of his shirt. The zipper of her dress slipped open as he worked on it, cool air brushing her skin in contrast to his warm fingers all the way down her back, but she refused to be sidetracked. Bane's defined pectorals were peeking out and she wanted to see the rest of what was under the fancy material.

"I haven't seen this set before," he said as her dress slid down her arms. "I'd have remembered this one."

Michaela shrugged the sleeves off to let it pool around her waist and continued to remove Bane's shirt. "No. This is the special occasion bra."

Finally. His bare chest. She paused to admire his understated muscles. No bulging veins or giant head-sized pecs here. No, his body made a wiry, chiseled V—widest at the shoulders and narrowing to rippling abdominals. So many interesting dips and ridges to explore. And he was all hers this evening. She sighed happily.

He snagged the lace-edged strap of her bra and tugged her closer. "Special occasion, as in the date you were set up on? Was Scott going to be able to see this set at any point?"

Since she was practically there anyway, she went ahead and straddled his lap. The hot jealousy in his tone made her the most desirable woman in the world. She pressed a kiss against the beat throbbing at the base of his throat. "Nope."

"Oh."

Another kiss, lower on his chest. "My mother inviting him along like a big third wheel doesn't make him a date. When I wear a nice dress I like to have something fancy underneath it." She kissed her way to the dark circle of his nipple. "So I feel special, for a special occasion." Spread over him like this, she was getting hotter and wetter by the second. The hard bulge of his cock rested right where she needed it, separated only by his dress slacks and her thin underwear.

"Good. You should always feel special." He stroked and soothed along her arms, over her shoulders, down her back. "Also the special occasion is me now. I'm just saying."

"I can agree to that." She caught his nipple between her lips, then blew on it. He sucked in a breath. The nurse part of her, which never turned off, noted he was favoring his bandaged hand and mostly using his other when he touched her. Good for him.

Gently he cupped her breasts, letting his thumbs trace the edges of the bra. She wondered idly if he could feel her heartbeat vibrating through the touch.

She trembled already, but he only teased, flirting with the edges of the soft material, dipping under the cup to brush a nipple, and then retreating. All the while he kept up the kisses, feathering them along her jaw, behind her ear.

"Bane," she moaned. "Please." She ground herself against him, empty and so ready to be filled.

He tensed. For one second, long enough for her to register it, he was frozen.

Then he breathed a word against her throat. "Hiro."

"What?" It sounded like *hee-do*, and she couldn't immediately identify which word he meant. She fought through the haze of arousal. "What hero?" Was there a superhero? Here in the building? Oh shit, had her mother sent UberMeta Man after them already?

"No, Hiro," he repeated. "My name. It's Hiro."

"You—your name?" She sat up straight and shoved her hair out of her face. "Your real name?"

"I want to hear my name, my actual name, if you're going to moan it like that." He gave her his typical, cocky Bane grin.

Except now she knew, he wasn't Bane. Tears pricked the corners of her eyes. "I wasn't moaning. Oh, Powers, how can you trust me like that?"

"I don't know. I just do." He wrapped firm arms around her and worked on the clasp of her bra. It loosened and slithered down her arms.

She laughed even as she ached. Her heart was blown wide open by his faith in her. "Hiro," she breathed. It wasn't perfectly as he'd pronounced it, but she tried. Gazing into his eyes, she vowed, "I'll never tell. I promise. Your secret's safe with me."

She buried her hands in his hair to pull him closer for a kiss. For a heartbeat she was furious at her power. She'd give anything to be able to touch him, really touch him, not just his hair, in a moment like this.

Chapter Eighteen

WHAT ARE YOU DOING, you idiot? Hiro didn't know. Even as he broke their kiss and bent to taste one of those perfect, pert nipples he had no idea.

Why would you tell her? Because he could trust her.

You don't know that! You barely know her. But he felt it.

No, your dick is feeling it. Do you seriously want to ruin everything you've built all these years? Screw up your revenge? This wouldn't ruin anything. She wanted to help people as much as he did. When she promised not to tell anyone, she meant it.

Michaela arched against his mouth, letting out a breathy gasp. Her hands tightened in his hair as he nipped and sucked. His cock pulsed, more than ready to be inside her. Pure need roared through him, driving him ruthlessly.

The blast of arousal was *almost* enough to drown out the doubts muttering inside his head. *You know what happens when you trust someone. When you* love *them, you always lose them.*

I'm not in love, he told himself, as he anchored her hips with his hands while he teased her other swollen, stiff nipple with his tongue. Just...extremely strong like. Super like. And admiration. And an incredible amount of lust.

She pressed her forearm to the back of his head and drew him up for another deep, searing kiss. His chest ached, as if it were expanding. Making room for her.

In love, each heartbeat thundered. *In love.*

Damn it. He couldn't even lie to himself.

He smoothed caressed the inside of her thighs. If the movement bothered his burn, he honestly didn't notice. So many other sensations were fighting for room, faint pain didn't stand a chance. Smooth, warm skin slid under his palms.

Michaela locked her arms around his neck, letting her legs fall open. Her nipples brushed against his bare chest.

Under the flowing cover of her dress, he found the edge of her panties. He tugged them aside with one hand so he could part the folds of her pussy with his thumb. She was all soft heat, and already soaking wet for him. Hiro groaned. He searched out the hard pearl of her clit and circled it gently with one slick finger until her hips started to buck.

He leaned back to enjoy the vision before him. Michaela's dark eyes met his, half lidded and full of hot need. Rich black hair tumbled over her bare shoulders in a riot of curls. She'd had it pinned up before. His hands had destroyed the careful arrangement, and the visible evidence of his touch was unbearably arousing. *Beautiful. So beautiful.*

Her skin flushed with a dusky rose undertone. Her lips parted just enough to let her sighs and pants escape as he worked her higher and higher. Her small, firm breasts bounced with each breath.

And she's all mine.

She pressed her lips to the sensitive skin above his collarbone and his whole body jerked in response. "I need to be inside you." In another time, he might have been embarrassed by the throaty rumble in his voice—how desperate he sounded. Right now, he didn't care, not while Michaela devoured him with nipping kisses and his hands kneaded the soft curves of her perfect ass.

"Yes. Please," she panted. She backed off his lap and stood to shimmy the dress over her hips and onto the floor. The lacy blue panties he'd already had his hands in matched her discarded bra, a color coordination he appreciated.

"You're gorgeous," he told her. "Look at those curves I get to touch." He stood to unfasten his pants while she consumed him with a gaze as intense as a caress. "Look how wet that special occasion underwear is."

She smirked, hooked her fingers in the waistband, and pulled them down. Then crooked a finger at him. "Get over here and make me even wetter."

"You're bossy too." How could he laugh, *and* crave so intensely at the same time? "I like it." His foot caught in the pile of pants and boxers around his ankle and he nearly stumbled in his hurry to get to her.

Arms lifted, she reached for him...and hesitated. Her brows drew together. "I can't touch you. I almost forgot." Wonder seeped into her tone. "I actually almost forgot."

"Why not? Why not touch me?" he asked. He gripped her hips and drew her flush against him, nipping at the corner of her lips.

"I've never put my hands on, um. Anyone. During. You know. I don't know what it would do." He slid his hands between them to cup her breasts, sending a shudder up her spine. "And your feelings are so strong I'm getting a taste of them now, just standing here. Combining the two? I don't know."

"I'm willing to test it." He pinched her nipples between thumbs and forefingers, rolling them into stiffer peaks. "I'll be the test subject."

"Ahh, fuck that feels good." She let out a breath. "I can't think. I'm not sure." Her expression was tortured.

Honestly, he could care less if she stopped his heart with the intensity of their feelings, but if it bothered her this much he wouldn't make her try it. Yet. "I've got this," he assured her.

She arched an eyebrow. "You do?"

In answer, he gripped her hips and spun her around. "Before I lose what's left of my mind...condom?" He was snug behind her, running his hands down her arms, smoothing, stroking. He lifted her wrists and placed her hands flat against the wall in front of her.

"No," she said breathlessly. She undulated her hips against him and he rewarded her bold move with a kiss on the curve of her neck. "I have the implant and I checked out clean on my last scan."

"I did too. And I replaced my implant last year," Hiro said. Since that was all taken care of, he reached around to find her breasts again. He alternated kisses between her neck, her shoulder, and her earlobe as he teased her nipples. Her fingers spasmed and tensed against the flat, white paint. By the time she began gasping, his cock leaked beads of pre cum against her ass.

"Hiro," she whimpered. "Inside. Me. Now." She arched her hips upwards, inviting him.

"Yes, please," he said. He gripped himself with one hand and slid the head of his cock through her wet folds, getting it nice and slick to slide in.

Finally, finally he eased the tip of his cock into her tight warmth. They groaned together.

Hiro's mind emptied, sensing nothing but his cock sliding into Michaela's warm, wet softness. He rocked slowly, teasing them both, working himself deeper until he was fully seated. Pressure, *pleasure*, held him in a merciless grip.

Her hips pressed back against him, urging him for more. With his bandaged hand, he gripped the curve of her waist, holding her still. With the other, he reached around and pressed a finger against the swollen clit begging for attention. Every pump into Michaela rubbed her against his finger, making her shudder. Nothing, nothing had ever felt so incredible.

Her lovely breasts needed attention. With one focused thought his power wrapped lightly around her, massaging tenderly. It was like having two additional hands, both devoted to her luscious body. Best part of his power, in his opinion.

"Hiro," she panted. "Oh, fuck, yes. Hiro."

Harder. He thrust in and out and she matched him beat for beat. Electric tingles danced up his spine, warning him how close he was to the edge.

Each time he thrust, she keened, trembling. It took every bit of his determination to hold on, to keep from spilling into that wet heat. Without enough focus his power fizzled out, and he lost his mental hold on her. He pressed two fingers against her clit, rubbing gently and she gave him a choked gasp.

"Hiro. Coming!"

Her back arched, then bowed as she tightened around his cock in pulsing waves.

"Yes," he hissed. "Michaela!"

He let himself go, let the pressure explode. Black starbursts filled his vision. Her orgasm surged with his, drawing the pleasure out. He banded his arm tightly around her chest, holding her to him as they shuddered together.

When the waves finally receded he sagged against her back, panting. Sweat stuck them skin to skin. He held on. If he had his way, he'd never let her go.

Everything in him wanted her. Trusted her. Needed her. He whispered a kiss against her shoulder and she shivered.

"Hiro."

"Mmmm?"

"Now we can make it to the bedroom."

"Okay." He didn't move.

She bucked her hips back against him. "Bedroom. Bed. My legs don't work."

"Good."

When she snickered, his heart throbbed. He wrapped both arms around her and took a few steps backward, keeping his cock inside her.

"Hiro. We can *not* walk all the way to the bedroom like this." She sounded so stern he grinned helplessly.

He spun them towards the short hallway and kept walking, step by careful step. She moved with him, giggling breathlessly.

"Seriously," she said. "We can't walk like this." Her curls streamed down her shoulders and back, tickling against his chest.

"We are walking like this." He wiggled his fingers at her waist, making her squirm. If they kept this up, he might be ready for another round in the bedroom. His cock stirred at the idea.

She must have felt it because she made a delicious little purring noise. A misstep in the hallway broke their rhythm and he had to slide out of her. At the doorway to her room she turned to lift an eyebrow at him. "See?"

All he saw was the most gorgeous naked woman in the world. Smiling at him. Rosy and flushed from his touches. He could have melted on the floor in a grateful heap. "Practice makes perfect," he told her firmly.

"Oh, well, in that case," she said, and stepped backward into the dark room.

Hiro rushed to follow.

Chapter Nineteen

THE PHONE ALARM TRILLED sweetly from Michaela's bedside table. She'd picked that tone on purpose because it sounded cheerful, but right this second the little trills made her wish for a meat mallet. She rolled over to slap at it and jolted to a stop when Hiro's arm tightened around her.

"Ugh. Hiro. My alarm," she rasped. He only squeezed her tighter.

She lunged for the phone, snatched it, and swiped away the annoying noise. Then she rolled to face her grabby bedmate, tossing the phone towards the end of the bed without caring where it landed.

He laid on his stomach, one arm stretched out to hold on to her. His face was buried in the pillow. Tufts of black hair puffed out at odd angles, so adorable she couldn't help the pinch it gave her heart.

"Morning," she said.

"Mmph."

"Time to get up." She slipped a kiss across his sleep warm shoulder. Light streamed in through her gauzy white curtain, highlighting the ridges and shadowing the valleys of his back. Tiny hairs at the nape of his neck shone. She barely resisted the urge to sift her fingers through them.

"Mmph. For you maybe." His voice was still rough with sleep. He shoved his head further into the pillow and yanked her closer.

"Hiro, it's Wednesday. I have to go to work." She said it mostly to convince herself. They'd spent the last two days, her days off, not moving far from her bed and it had been *wonderful*. Michaela sighed and snuggled closer to his side, enjoying the soft slide of the blanket and the warmth of his body against her naked skin.

Before she had a hint of his intentions he rolled and hugged her to his chest. He caught her lips in a luxurious, indulgent kiss that tied her up in slippery sweet knots. She wrapped her arm around his neck and held on.

100

Just when she'd decided to call in sick, he pulled away and rubbed his nose against hers. His eyes were still closed. "Okay. Now you can go to work," he said.

She snorted out a laugh. "And you'll just go back to sleep?"

"Best part of being a supervillain? Waking up whenever you want." He traced lazy patterns up and down her bare back.

"You don't...have things to do today?" Part of her hesitated to ask, on the chance he kept all of his work a secret.

What did he do during the day? He kept track of upcoming battles; she knew that. When he fought Furia he always had some sort of extremely advanced tech, so he probably created and tinkered. Sometimes he battled other superheroes. And...he probably did a lot of computer type stuff? She really had no idea how any of it worked. How did he make enough money to pay bills?

Who was Hiro when he wasn't being The Evil Bane?

One of his eyes cracked open, enough for the black of his iris to peek out. "I do have some chores that need to get done today."

"Top-secret kind of things?" she asked tentatively.

He frowned, but it looked more thoughtful than irritated. "No. Not really secret. I just haven't had anyone interested in talking about my day in...years. Not someone I could actually *tell*." He closed his eye and settled back on the pillow.

Her whole heart wobbled. She tucked her head beneath his chin and nuzzled his neck. Every bit of her wanted to take the loneliness from him, suck it out, and throw it away and never let him feel like that again. "I'm interested."

When he chuckled, it rumbled delightfully in her ear. "I know you are. Mostly I have to monitor my surveillance. Sift through stuff to listen for hints of a big battle coming up. Do lots of emailing, maybe a little hacking. Tinker with my toys. Experiment to make new ones."

She thought back to the urgent care, the moment she'd—*let's just admit it*—nearly kissed him. When she'd asked what happened, he'd answered with something like *spearmint.* Spearmint. Experiment. "That's what you did to your arm? Were you tinkering with a laser?"

Both of his eyes opened and he cast her a surprised look. "Anyone ever tell you you're exceptionally quick and intuitive?"

"Yes. Mrs. Fish."

"Well, she was right." His gaze shifted to her bedside table and he smiled. "Hey, you kept the rose."

"Oh. Yeah. I did." The glass cup she'd tucked her flower into magnified and refracted the colors dancing along the petals, splashing rainbows across her bedside table.

Michaela's glance caught the red numbers on the clock sitting next to her rose. "Shit!" She flung herself backward. "Crap!" In one surge she tossed the blanket down and shoved herself out of bed.

Hiro fought his way out of the blanket, lost his balance, and seized the headboard to keep from tumbling to the floor. "What? What's after us?" He flung out one hand. The door slammed shut in a gust of potenkinesis. His raised his other hand to cover the window next to him and the curtains billowed.

Halfway to the bathroom she paused. "Nothing's after us."

His hands were up at a ready-to-kill angle while he crouched to spring, completely naked. The threatening pose was ruined only a little by his dangling bits.

She bit the inside of her cheek, hard. First rule of dating: *no one* wants to hear laughter when they're standing in front of you bare-assed naked. "Sorry. Sorry. No threat. Stand down. I'm going to be late for work."

Slowly, he straightened. "Oh. Right."

He ran a hand through his tousled hair, looking sheepish. His muscles pulled taut from waist to shoulder in captivating ways. Michaela's throat dried up and she licked her lips.

"Need a shower? I can join you." He ran a warm gaze from her toes to her head and back.

Honey-sweet lust rolled through her. She desperately wished for his fingers inside her. "If it's *really* quick."

He sauntered over. "Some things we should not rush. But I can be efficient."

Chapter Twenty

FIFTEEN MINUTES LATER, Hiro let Michaela tug her hand from his. He watched her rush down the hallway and sighed. She did have to work. And he did have all sorts of things to accomplish today.

His arms didn't want to let her go. His body missed her warmth snuggled up against it. Even his dick rebelled at the idea of being away from her for endless, eternal hours. Every cell in his brain threw a teeny tantrum, missing her soft voice and her laugh. He could go after her, tug her back into her apartment and talk her into staying home. He'd find that spot that made her purr if he curled his finger just right...

Hiro scrubbed a hand over his eyes.

Addiction. Is this what it felt like? This constant craving?

Instead of opening the apartment door to gather his things, he leaned his head against it and banged once or twice. The Evil Bane was hooked on a sidekick. Her mother, a superhero, would like to flame broil his guts. Her father, probably also superpowered, could show up to ask the *ow-pain* kind of questions about dating his daughter any day now.

If he were really unlucky Michaela's parents would set Smallcity's Legion Chapter on him. The Legion of Associated Superheroes could come after him with anything from a fine accompanied by a verbal warning, to imprisonment in a Super Max, or exile in another dimension.

He hadn't heard of someone on the side of Evil *ever* dating someone from the Good. Which meant the Legion wouldn't have the first idea what to do about it or what penalties to try imposing on him. Hopefully. But knowing them and their absolute rigidity for sticking to the rules...they'd come up with something.

This could not end well. But he couldn't stop. He didn't care if Furia and the entire Legion all came after him at once. He would do anything to have Michaela stay.

Footsteps echoed from the stairwell. He turned to look at the empty doorway as his tantruming cells started cheering, sure they were about to get their Michaela fix.

Utterly fucking addicted.

"Wipe off that smile, boy, it's only me," Mrs. Fish said as she emerged. She strolled down the hallway towards number 405, a shopping bag dangling from her crooked elbow.

"Can't I be glad to see you?" He leaned against Michaela's door and crossed his arms, his stomach still leaping happily.

"Not *that* much, thank you. Save it for my darling girl. How was dinner Monday night?"

Hiro threw up his hands and flung his head back. "Do you know everything? What do I even do my job for when I could just ask you?" he demanded the ceiling.

She nudged him with her elbow. When he looked at her, she gave him a smirk. "Simmer down, Evil Bane. Michaela texted me. She said you showed up instead of her mother's hand-picked date. Congratulations on a well-played trick, there. And I think we should talk if you've got some time."

He did recall Michaela tapping on her phone during one of their breaks over the last two days. "Talk? A heavy, what-are-your-intentions, kind of talk?"

"No, not so much. More of a things-you-really-should-know talk. And I'll sweeten the deal. I'll make you breakfast." She raised her eyebrows challengingly. "I'm just down the hall."

"Then it's a deal." Hiro nodded and followed her, absolutely seduced by the promise of more insight about Michaela.

Inside apartment 422, Mrs. Fish produced a carton of eggs, some spinach, tomatoes. And—sweet Powers above he might also fall in love with Mrs. Fish—cinnamon rolls.

"So, let's hear about dinner," she prompted.

His mouth watered as he watched her work. "Dinner was tense. I'm forbidden to see or date Michaela. I'm too much of a softy snowflake about villains and I had the nerve to say superheroes cause unnecessary deaths in their enthusiasm. There was a not-subtle threat about calling in her father. Do you know who he is?"

"Of course." She nodded. From the top of her fridge she acquired a plastic cutting board and started dicing tomatoes.

Hiro waited for her to expand on that. And waited. He opened cupboards at random, trying to find coffee or mugs. And kept waiting.

Mrs. Fish nodded towards a bottom cabinet, which turned out to be her pantry.

"Oooh. Good stuff." He admired the bag of organic dark roast. "Are you going to *tell* me who Michaela's dad is? I mean, which superhero?"

"Nope. Mugs are in that cabinet." Tomatoes done, she sloshed olive oil in a skillet and threw in the spinach.

After Hiro grabbed two mugs he examined the ancient percolator on Mrs. Fish's countertop. He regularly created complex, multi-system nanotechnology for use in major battles. He *would not* be defeated by a twenty-year-old coffee maker. "Do you make Michaela breakfast every morning?"

As he dumped the water inside the machine he realized it was the wrong side of the reservoir. Most of the water splashed onto the counter. "Shit." He unplugged the thing, emptied it out, and tried again.

"Boy, she is twenty-two years old. I don't her make breakfast every day." The oil sizzled, the spinach began to wilt. She dropped the tomatoes in, grabbed a bowl from the cabinet above her, and cracked eggs into it.

"She's twenty-two?" Hiro could practically *feel* his eyes pop into cartoon heart shapes. "I'm twenty-eight. In case you were wondering."

Mrs. Fish nodded. "That's good. Michaela and I usually make breakfast together on Monday mornings. Celebrate her day off, you know? Set the table, please."

He nodded. When he flicked the worn-off switch he hoped was the *on* button, the percolator coughed and wheezed.

"I invited you over for breakfast this morning because I'm nosy," Mrs. Fish informed him, whisking with brisk, firm movements. "I wanted to know what went wrong with dinner. I wanted to know if I need to be watching for her dad, which it sounds like I do. And I like you."

"You do?" Hiro smiled as he got plates out of another cupboard, ridiculously pleased. He'd worry about Michaela's dad later.

"Michaela is all heart. No backbone. You're all balls. No heart. I think each of you is what the other one needs. You balance each other."

"Well that's...blunt. But probably a good way to put it." He pursed his lips. Was Michaela his heart? Would she make him softer? She might. And he would gladly be her backbone. "Can I ask how you know Michaela so well? It's pretty obvious you're her real mom. When you get down to what matters."

She beamed at him, nearly blinding him with her smile. "Now that's a nice thing to say." She tipped the eggs on top of the veggies, left them to cook, and opened the box of cinnamon rolls to scoop them onto a plate. "You've figured out by now that Michaela's parents are both superheroes."

She'd made a statement, not asked a question, but he nodded anyway. The coffee maker *blatted*. He glared at it.

"They stayed busy. Too busy saving the world to take care of a daughter. After it was clear they couldn't handle both they advertised for a live-in nanny. And they got me."

It all made so much sense now. "When did you discover you both had the same power?"

"The same day I came to take care of her. First time I hugged that baby girl, standing there with her big, sad eyes. You're sharp, aren't you." She flashed a narrow look at him. "How'd you know?"

Hiro shrugged. "She touched your hand. She won't do that with me unless I talk her into it and she *never* touches anyone else. With you, she doesn't even think twice. It just makes sense that she'd be so comfortable with someone who shared the same power." He tried not to envy that, but it wasn't easy.

Mrs. Fish sagged a little, as if reminded of a heavy load forever perched on her shoulders. "It's been pounded into her head that it's bad. Her own parents didn't know how to handle her power, and they couldn't exactly hide their aversion from her. There's no shield against feelings." She sighed heavily. "When someone can know all of you, everything you try to hide with a single touch, it's invasive. It's frightening. Empaths, we aren't welcome."

He straightened up from where he'd been setting down forks. "Empaths. That's what it's called? I'd never even heard of it before."

"Empaths is what we are. Empathy is the word for the power. We don't come out much." Her smile hung crooked, so full of ache it hurt him. "Do you know how much pure hate there is in the world? How much pain and misery? Just as no one can shield against us, *we* can't shield against them. All it takes is one accidental touch. And once they figure out what we can do—when they start fearing us or depending on our help like a drug—it's worse. A lot of us avoid other humans all together and being cut off from everyone and everything like that is...awful. No contact. Total isolation. No *touch*. It gets to be too much to take."

"No. Wait. No." He thumped his hand down on the top of the table. The plates rattled. "That will *never* happen to Michaela. Anything she needs to get through, I'll do it. I'll find a shield that works. I'll *be* her shield. I love her. I love what she can do."

Mrs. Fish paused, her hands full with the skillet of scrambled eggs, and raised both eyebrows.

The realization of what he'd said slammed into him. *Okay. Way to blurt out everything in your head, Hiro. Great.* He pinned his disloyal lips together and shifted a plate back from the edge of the table. He might not have meant to just...explode his feelings all over the place, but he meant every word. Not one would be taken back.

"I knew I liked you." She plunked the food down and turned back to get the cinnamon rolls out of the microwave. "Sit down and eat."

He settled carefully into a chair, picked up his fork, and just stared at it. "Don't...don't tell Michaela. I'll tell her myself." She'd feel it for herself, the next time she touched him.

"No need for me to *say* a thing. That's part of the problem with us Empaths." Mrs. Fish echoed his own thought while she nudged the plate of cinnamon rolls closer to him. "Are you sure you can handle it?"

"I'm not *sure*. But I want to find out if I can."

"Fair enough," she admitted. "Eat up."

Chapter Twenty One

"IVAN," MICHAELA SAID warningly. "Hey! That's mine." She couldn't help laughing as his arm tightened around her, pinning her in place long enough to snatch a bite. "If you wanted mint chocolate chip, why didn't you just get some yourself?"

In public, he had to go by 'Ivan'. She wouldn't give up his secret for anything. And, luckily, using an alter-ego name outside the house was already habit for her. She snuck a quick kiss to the side of his mouth while he was trying to escape.

"Don need to. I c'n just share with you," he said thickly through his stolen mouthful. He swallowed. "Want some of mine?"

Her nose scrunched. "No. Nuts are not supposed to go in ice-cream. It's gross."

"Your loss." He took a long, slow, exaggerated lick of his own cone. "Mmmm. Pistachio. Yummy."

"They're *salty*." She shuddered.

Hiro laughed and tugged her closer to press a kiss against her temple, more relaxed than she'd ever seen him. He looked at her like...like she'd hung the sun and turned the sky blue, just because she knew blue was his favorite color. If it were possible she'd capture that look to keep forever, to wrap herself up in it like a warm blanket.

The Riverwalk stretched ahead, winding through downtown Smallcity. Soft green spread to each side of the concrete walk, a palette made of bushes, lawns, and trees. Artfully placed flower beds flashed little rainbows of color. Chunky, carved stone benches sat at intervals for walkers to rest. Sunset gleamed between the giant buildings towering in front of them, highlighting the edges and shadowing the sides.

Michaela couldn't remember having a better day off. Ever. Unless she was thinking of the carnival two weeks ago, but that had ended badly. To say the least. Today? Today was perfect.

For most of the week she and Hiro had only seen each other after work. Okay, he'd spent every night at her apartment, but it didn't feel like enough time. Now that her irregular weekend had finally started they'd spent all day together, starting off at Monday breakfast with Mrs. Fish. Michaela had been amazed and delighted at the casual ease between her boyfriend and her heart's mother. She didn't have to smooth over any rough patches. Mrs. Fish didn't have to pretend a thing. She actually liked him.

She'd completed all her house chores while Hiro worked on the laptop he'd brought from his...place. She couldn't say for sure if it was his villain lair, a decoy home—or just an innocent apartment. She hadn't seen it, and she tried to shove down her curiosity. Hiro would show her his personal space when he was ready. When he trusted her. Since he hadn't invited her home yet she had a suspicion it was his lair, and *that* was a reveal to take seriously.

They'd shopped for groceries for the week. Hiro ascribed to the *death before dishonor* school of carrying bags, while she was more the *as many trips as it takes* type. After arguing cheerfully about it while putting everything away in her apartment, they'd come here for the most beautiful evening walk by the river. With ice cream.

Best of all—Hiro wasn't intimidated by her Empathy. He'd found a solution that was so incredibly, unbelievably *simple* she couldn't believe it had never occurred to her before.

Hiro used his words.

If he felt a need for privacy, *he said so*. On the rare occasions he'd had a bad day he would tell her and ask not to be touched bare-handed for a little while. When he'd managed his own emotions, like a mature adult, he'd let her know it was okay to touch him again. And somehow, it all worked beautifully.

Years and years, a *lifetime* of feeling unwanted and intrusive, had tangled into a thicket of pain and rejection and defensiveness and a compulsive need to wear gloves all the time. And her supervillain had cut a smooth path through it all in seconds with a few *words*.

She didn't think she could ever convey to him how much that meant to her, but she could try.

Michaela wrapped her arm more firmly around Hiro's waist and took another bite of her ice-cream. Aside from a stiff, short phone call yesterday, she hadn't heard from Furia. There was no sign of UberMeta Man against the melted orange sunset. For a little while longer, she could pretend everything would be fine.

Against her side, Hiro stiffened. Then he gripped her tight and ducked towards the nearest tree, dragging her along.

"What's wrong?" she whispered as they ran. Who was after them? Had someone recognized him? Surely not. She scanned the sky, again. Nothing.

"Look," he whispered. "Right there." He indicated the direction with one hand. "Red shirt. Blue jeans. Is that Velocity?"

She peered around the knobbed tree trunk. "Velocity? As in, Captain Champion's sidekick?" Her voice stayed a bare thread. Bane obviously didn't want to be caught, whatever they were doing.

"That's the one. You know him, right?"

"Yes, I know him. I think that's him." As if feeling their gaze, the figure on the Riverwalk turned to scan the path behind him and she got a good look at his face. A sweep of high cheekbones, stubby nose, dark blond hair. A worried, tense expression. "Yes. That's Velocity. Why?"

The sidekick faced forward again and continued walking, slowly. His hands were tucked into the pockets of his jeans and his shoulders slumped.

"Yes! Finally," Hiro hissed. "Stay here." He tucked his mostly-finished cone into her free hand. After checking his pocket, he frowned and dug out his wallet. "Can you hold this for me, too? Just in case? I think I'll have to run hard."

"Um, sure?" She had to juggle the two cones with his wallet. Distracted, she didn't notice he'd pulled out a thin slide of black material until he swirled it up and over his head.

The material flowed around him, covering his head, shoulders, and torso. Hiro reached inside the deep hood and pulled down—*light tubes*. Flexible, thin strands of bright red. They framed the edge of the hood in a vicious, techno gash.

Two softball-sized circles surrounded each of his eyes, with a brilliant cutting X across the middle. A line of slashes marched crosswise, just over his nose. The whole effect was vaguely skull-like, in a high tech, menacing way.

The Evil Bane was coming out to play.

"What are you doing?" she demanded. The bottom of her ice cream cone shattered beneath her tight grip and cold slithered over her fingers. Mint sharpened the air.

"I've been trying to get my hands on Veloxity for *years*," he murmured. His grin, that familiar, reckless Bane grin, flashed from underneath the lights of his mask. "Little shit is so damn fast. I'll get him this time." He tugged black gloves over his hands.

"Get him for *what*? Why?"

He was gone.

Cursing steadily under her breath, Michaela tossed both cones in the direction of a trash can, wiped her hand off on her jeans, and dashed after The Evil Bane. She tucked Hiro's wallet safely in her pocket.

Ahead of her, Veloxity—Chris, in his normal life—walked on. Completely unaware. Should she shout at him, warn him? What was The Evil Bane planning for him?

Veloxity was a friend. They'd sat together during endless, boring Legion meetings, trading memes on their cell phones and snorting until Captain Champion glared them both quiet. When the Smallcity

Chapter brought her promotion to sidekick to a vote he'd voted *aye*, in her favor.

She bolted towards her friend. "*Chris*," she whisper-hissed. No civilians were in sight. The Riverwalk stretched on, open and empty in the growing twilight. She couldn't see Bane anywhere.

"Chris!" she shouted.

He spun around. "Amia–I mean, Michaela? What's wrong?"

Her breath came in quick spurts. "Chris, be careful." She slid to a stop in front of him and scanned their surroundings desperately, dancing from foot to foot.

Who should she betray? Her friend and fellow sidekick, or her boyfriend?

"You're in trouble. The–The E–" she couldn't get the words out. Her throat closed on the treachery. "Just run!"

Chris had the power to move like a strip of flesh-colored light. Quicker than any car, any jet, any engine. Undoubtedly the reason The Evil Bane hadn't been able to catch him yet.

But Chris didn't listen to her and turn on the speed. He only stood there looking confused. "Who's after you? What's going on, Michaela?" One hand crept towards his pocket.

"Not me! After you. Go!" She nearly shoved him to get him going. Stubborn idiot!

"Someone's after me? Who?" Chris tensed, leaning toward her.

"Me," said The Evil Bane, gleefully, from behind him. "Hello, Veloxity."

Instead of turning into a human colored streak and disappearing around the nearest building, Chris turned around. He squared up. To fight. Did he *want* to be caught?

His hand came out of his pocket at what looked like glacial speed to Michaela. She had more than enough time to catalog every detail.

Before her eyes had finished registering the shape of the blaster, Michaela burst into a run.

When the white energy beam cut through the air, Michaela was already where she wanted to be. In front of Bane. It bounced off her shoulder, shoving her back a step. She stiffened her back and stood firm.

"Michaela, shit, I'm sorry—move!" Chris shouted. He raised the blaster again. "It's Evil Bane!"

She rolled her eyes so hard her chin tipped back.

Bane flung his arm over her shoulder with his fingers spread. She *felt* the potenkinesis brush by her cheek. He'd thrown something. She barely saw it moving as it leapt to Chris.

Michaela stared at her friend, horrified. What had Bane hit him with?

He jerked, stumbling forward a step. "Michaela, what—" His eyelids fluttered. Finally, she spotted the black dot clinging to the side of his neck. He gulped once, twice, and the blaster fell to the ground. She covered her mouth with one shaky hand.

Chris crashed onto the grass.

Michaela whirled on Bane. "What did you do?"

"He's fine. What the fuck were you thinking? Are you hurt?" Bane spun her around to scan her from top to bottom. He gently tugged the scoop-neck of her shirt to the side, looking for the burned, smoking hole a blaster should leave.

There was nothing. Her skin was smooth and unmarked. Of course.

He frowned. "Did he miss you? From that close? Dammit, Michaela, I thought he got you dead on." Behind the pulsing red light, his gaze shifted to the downed sidekick. He snarled.

He did get me dead on. It's fine. Part of her wanted to tell him. Part of her was reacting from the gut, seeing that mask facing her. Her fingers twitched. She could reach inside, find terror, blind panic, touch him bare-handed, shove them into him...

"What. Did you do. To Chris," she asked again, through gritted teeth. She squeezed her hands into fists at her side.

He sighed and patted her shoulder lightly. "Tranquilizer. Instant tranquilizer, I should say." He walked to the sidekick sprawled in the grass, bent over, and tapped the side of the dot clinging to Velocity's neck.

It detached and crept up his arm into his sleeve. Like a bug. A spider.

A microbot. The Evil Bane specialized in bots of all sizes. She should have remembered. Michaela dropped to her knees by her friend and leaned down to listen to his breathing. His respiration was steady and sounded smooth. She pulled a pair of nitrile gloves out of her back pocket and tugged them on.

"Will it hurt him?" The pulse in his wrist was steady under her fingers. She let out a breath, slightly reassured, and lifted his hand to just above chest height.

"No, it won't hurt him. He'll sleep for, ah, twelve to fifteen hours." Bane waved his hand sideways to indicate the time variation. "Why are you...squeezing Velocity's finger?"

"CRT," she murmured vaguely.

"You know I have no idea what that means," Bane said.

"I'm checking his circulation." She had distracted Velocity. This was her fault. Bane might have even counted on her trying to warn Velocity, keeping him busy. She had helped capture another sidekick.

Whose side am I on now? Oh, Powers, whose side?

Gently, she felt the back of her fellow sidekick's head. At least he'd fallen onto good soft grass. She couldn't feel a hematoma forming. Not yet, anyway.

"How's his head?"

"Fine, I think."

Bane shrugged. "I won't dose him again. I won't hurt him, I promise. I really need him, alive and well." He bent to get an arm underneath Chris. "Will you help me get him up off the ground? I've got to get him to the lair."

"Why? To do what?" She wrapped her arms around Chris and staggered to her feet as Bane hauled up the unconscious man's torso. Each of them took an arm around their necks to steady his dead weight.

They might have been escorting a drunk friend safely home from the bar. Except it was a Monday evening. And The Evil Bane, decked out in all his tech, lurked at her side.

Her stomach hurt. Her friend, or her boyfriend? Turned out it was her boyfriend. The superheroes, or the supervillain? Her heart, her instincts, reacted before her brain had a say. Supervillain won. And this path couldn't be unmade. If she chose to help him knock out and kidnap a sidekick, if she willingly walked into his lair as part of this plot...

Bane cleared his throat. "Bait. I'm going to use him as bait. I needed a way to get Captain Champion to come to me. He's the last one I haven't battled in Smallcity. Well, almost the last one." She thought he shuddered a little, but she couldn't be sure.

"You *want* a battle with Captain Champion?" Stupid. Of course he did. He battled heroes. *Because he was a supervillain.*

"Yes. And this is your chance, Michaela. If you don't want to be a part of this, I get it. You didn't sign up for supervillain work. You're a *sidekick*. The Legion isn't going to like this. Walk away now, I'll understand completely. I can...get my wallet later, after I've tucked Veloxity away somewhere safe." His voice vibrated with intensity, but she couldn't name the emotion driving it.

They took a few steps, adjusting to the weight. Chris's head bobbed loosely, and she nudged it to rest on Bane's shoulder so he wouldn't hurt himself more by flopping around. A tiny bit of drool escaped the corner of his mouth.

Michaela's thoughts bounced. From *yes* to *no* and back again. She *was* a sidekick—helping a supervillain abduct one of her side. She trusted Bane. Hiro. He wouldn't hurt Chris. Whatever his plan included for Captain Champion, he must have a reason to battle him.

I hope. I mean, I hope he's got a reason. Beyond 'I want to kill all superheroes.'

She wasn't a villain. If she did this, she'd be shifting to that side. They'd been dating a few weeks. Enough time to change the trajectory of your entire life for a lover? Yeah, no.

But he was right when he accused superheroes of causing as much damage as supervillains. She knew it, had always known it, and shoved the knowledge away. Bane did more than nursing, cleaning up the broken messes the Empowered left behind. His methods might not be the most legal, but he actively tried to make sure those battles never hurt anyone in the first place. *That* was the side she wanted to be on, even if it came with a side of villain.

She loved that fierce, protective part of him. She...loved him.

You're an idiot. Furia is going to bring you before the Legion Chapter for this, you know that, right? Full Tribunal. She'll try to separate us. She might even push for exile to another dimension. Not to mention what dad will do? She knew it.

She would face it, whatever came, to stand beside Hiro for something she believed in.

He seemed to be holding his breath, staring at the sidewalk like one wrong move would walk them all into a landmine.

"Let's get him to your lair. I'm coming." she said, grimly.

"Really? You're sure?" He sounded so surprised. Stunned, even. And happy. It was jarring for Michaela to hear those tones come from behind that mask.

"I'm sure. And *I'm* taking care of Veloxity while we wait for Captain Champion."

Chapter Twenty Two

FOR SEVERAL LONG, DUMBFOUNDED, seconds, Michaela just stood there. Mouth open. Closed. Open again. Finally, she sucked in some air. "E.B. Industries?"

From the sidewalk two steps away, where he sagged under Veloxity's weight, Hiro waited. She'd dropped her portion of the burden when she realized which building they were walking into.

Before they left the Riverwalk he'd tugged back his hood, hiding the mask of The Evil Bane. He kept the black cloak, with the many hidden pockets, though. Probably swarming with nanobots.

"E.B. Industries?" she asked again. She raised both hands to cover her eyes and groaned. "E.B. Eee-Bee. Evil Bane."

"Yep." Impatiently, he shifted from side to side. A stray lock of hair bobbed into his eye and he huffed at it. "You've got it. Now, can you get over here and help me again?" He scowled at the blond head sagging against his chest. "For such a small man he's built like a brick."

Michaela shook her head again. "I can't believe no one's ever figured it out. It's so *simple*. Powers, it's the thinnest cover I've ever heard of. Sharon should have got it the second she said SCB was interested."

"Hey. Hey. Not *the* thinnest. What about Water Wonder and his mutant lobster farm? *Everyone* knows it's his."

"It's your initials. Your damn initials," she said. "Oh, my Powers, I can't believe this."

Hiro hop-stepped over to her and grabbed her wrist. "I can't hold him up much longer. Especially not out in the open on a downtown sidewalk. Come. Inside." He tugged hard enough to make her sway.

Still numb with shock, she followed him. She examined the building once more, tilting her head back. Black and shining, it soared above them, a sharp, acute triangle coming to a brutal point. Faint red letters flashed high at the top. It hulked, looming over the street. A few people walked by, barely glancing at this city landmark. They probably saw it every day. Just another building downtown.

Michaela frowned. For a moment she thought she'd seen a flash of blonde hair in a perfectly asymmetrical cut. Just a glimpse as the person whipped around the corner of E.B. Industries. *Sharon? Why would Sharon be downtown?* No. Plenty of women had short blonde hair. It had to be someone else.

She shook her head and followed her supervillain into his lair.

The doors *whooshed* shut behind her. Sleek and silver, a counter ran the length of the lobby. Nobody sat behind it. Gargantuan golden-bronze numbers spread in a circle, with sharp-tipped arrows delineating the time. The ridiculously huge clock took up nearly the whole wall across from the entrance. From two stories above them, square lights dangled in an ultra-modern boxy arrangement.

Self-service kiosks ranged against the wall to both sides of the main entrance, a precise row of matte-black boxy soldiers. No one used them now, late on a Monday evening. But she knew they bustled with activity during the day. She'd used them herself to pay her first few months of rent.

"You *own* E.B. Industries?" she asked—just to make sure.

"Ah, yes. Yes, I do." Hiro huffed from over by the elevator doors. The light gleamed off their shiny ebony surface. "Give me a hand here?"

"Sorry." She hurried to his side and draped Chris's arm over her neck. She shifted, settling back into bearing the weight. "You're *obsessed* with the color black. You know that?"

"Doesn't stain easily." Hiro shrugged one shoulder.

The doors slid open, and they dragged Chris inside. His sneakers squeaked across the highly polished floor.

Hiro pressed his thumb against a completely bare section of wall above the lighted number panel. It beeped and popped open, revealing *another* circle. The ordinary panel went up to number nineteen. This hidden one contained only a single floor, number twenty.

It had to be his secret lair.

Faint muzak drifted from the speakers. It was almost, but not quite, recognizable, tugging at her memory. And the rhythm changed every few bars. After a few seconds she wanted to cover the speakers with a blanket.

"Out of curiosity, how is Captain Champion going to know you have his sidekick?" She shifted, trying to keep Chris level. His arm slid along her sweaty neck. "Assuming he doesn't have a tracker on him?"

"I'll make my standard video. You know, low threatening laughter and a scary swivel chair. Blinky lights. Fog machine. Tesla coils. Stroking my cat menacingly."

Her lips twisted into a reluctant smile. "It's so cliché. And, you know, swivel chairs aren't inherently threatening. Not really."

"It's my very favorite part. I *love* making menacing videos."

When the elevator slid to a stop at the twentieth floor, they stepped out to a hallway paved in shiny black. The doors that ran along the corridor were painted the same dark, metallic gray as the walls and bare of any decoration. All in all, Hiro's lair had the cheer of a gothic-modern hospital at midnight during a new moon.

Hiro guided their awkward trio to the closest door. He pressed a thumb to the side of it, and it beeped before sliding up and disappearing into the ceiling.

"Thumb-locks everywhere." Michaela raised her eyebrows. "Super high tech."

"Well, yeah." He indicated a twin-sized bed in the center of the room with a jerk of his head. "It's my thing." Slowly, they lowered Chris onto the fluffy gray blanket. He was snoring softly. The worry lines had smoothed out of his face in sleep.

Aside from the bed, the room was plain. Bare walls. Bare floor. A small alcove she assumed must lead to a bathroom. No window. The Evil Bane obviously had a utilitarian approach to kidnapped sidekicks.

Hiro straightened and rolled his shoulders, grumbling a little. He tugged his cloak up to look at his wrist where a rectangular display about the size of a phone screen flashed across the back of his glove. "Scanners checked him as we came in, and in the elevator. He doesn't have a tracker. He does have two more blasters on him." He bent to extract them; one from a small holster at his side, one from around his ankle.

As Hiro tucked them away somewhere inside his cloak he shook his head, sadly. "For a fast little fucker he sure packs a lot of firepower. He's got trust issues." He turned to stare at Michaela, raking his gaze from her head to her feet. "You're *sure* he missed you?"

She shrugged, pulling her shirt aside so he could see her shoulder again. "He must have. See?"

Hiro stepped closer. "Not really. Don't see how he could have missed from that distance. He's got trust issues and *terrible* aim." He wrapped his arms around her and kissed her temple. "Do not do that again. Okay? Don't even try to take shots meant for me. I've got shields. I'll be fine. You don't have anything."

She smiled. He didn't know what she had. He genuinely worried for her. It was sweet. "I promise. Unless your life is in direct danger. Okay?"

"Mmph," he grunted.

"That's my condit—" A small sound, a cross between a *mew* and a *mrrt* sounded behind her. Michaela spun around. "What in hells is that?"

She gaped at the open doorway and the little, pink, wrinkly blob sitting within. The blob watched her with greenish, luminous eyes.

Hiro started, then sagged in relief. "Purriarty. My supervillain accessory. He's a sphinx cat."

"That is not a cat. That's an inside-out vagina with ears. And a tail."

He stared at her with his mouth half open for a little while. Finally, he said, "Well, thanks for that fun mental image. I will now be unable to pet my poor cat, for the rest of his life, without thinking about the words *petting* and *pussy*. And *pink*." His voice sounded choked. "That's a terrible thing to do to a supervillain accessory."

Michaela shrugged.

Purriarty eyed her narrowly for a moment, then stood. As if it were an accident, or like random currents in the air propelled him, he drifted over to twine around Hiro's legs. Then he flashed her another long stare.

"The inside-out vagina likes you," Hiro said.

"Mm-hmm. I'm thrilled. Go make your video, or whatever you need to do. But show me where the kitchen is, first. I'll get Veloxity a glass of water."

"Why?" Hiro reached down and scratched Purriarty's bald head, absently. Then he glanced at his fingers and grimaced.

"He'll probably have dry mouth from whatever tranquilizer you used. When he wakes up." She frowned. "A headache too...do you have a medicine cabinet? I'd also like to know what's in your tranquilizer formula so I can figure out how people might react to it." She reached down to check her friend's pulse again. Still strong and steady.

He held out a hand. "Come on. He's fine. I'll show you where everything is."

"I'm in The Evil Bane's secret lair." She shook her head and moved to follow her supervillain. "Inside. I can barely believe it."

Chapter Twenty Three

HIRO SETTLED INTO HIS favorite spiky swivel chair. He'd worked long and hard to make it look terrifying, like shards of volcanic glass rearing at his back and sides. Framing and reflecting the harsh red light of his mask. In this case, a swivel chair could *absolutely* be inherently threatening.

The scary chair finished with a comfy cushion for his ass, which the camera would never see.

He patted his lap gently. Purriarty jumped up and settled on top of his thighs. Not without digging his claws in and kneading his leg a bit first, of course. He waited patiently for his cat to settle down, checking video angles.

The first few times Hiro had recorded one of these, he hadn't anticipated a felines' natural urge to be a little bastard. He'd had to re-shoot every time, because he couldn't send out an intimidating video where the villain was wincing and cursing at his cat and shoving him off his lap every few seconds.

Michaela was nowhere to be seen. Presumably, she was still getting Veloxity his recovery kit, which she would leave on the floor with a little note. The sidekicks he kidnapped to force their hero into a confrontation did not get the consideration of a note. Why explain anything when everyone, including the sidekick, already knew the procedure? But Hiro was in too good a mood to care.

She's here. She's really here. Michaela picked me. He could show her his experiments. Brag about the scary chair. Tour the lair with her. He could show her everything. Tell her anything.

At the Riverwalk, he'd been bracing himself to lose her. *Walk away now, I'll understand completely* he'd said, but inside he'd been begging *pick me, choose me. Don't leave me.*

And she'd stayed.

Carefully, he chased and caught every butterfly trembling inside his stomach, trapping each one away inside his heart. Supervillains did not grin like goofy besotted idiots. Or have shiny love eyes. Supervillains definitely did not have a raging hard on in videos they would send to their enemies.

Okay. Okay. Ready. Hiro thumbed the button set into the arm of his chair. He stared into the blinking eye of his camera, his expression blank behind the lights of his mask. Letting the suspense build.

"Captain Champion," he said, finally. His mouth curled into a sneer. Powers, he loved doing his job. Loved knowing how helpless the arrogant Captain would feel watching this.

"I have something which belongs to you." He would edit in a video clip of the hero's sidekick snoring on the bed in the bare containment room before he sent the video.

Stroking Purriarty with his forefinger, he fought down the extremely distracting mental image Michaela had planted. Oh, he was going to spank her for that later. He firmed his lips, keeping the smirk mean. Not sexy.

Speaking of the cat-petting-wrecker, she had just slipped into the room and was now standing just behind the camera tripod, mouth curled into an amused smile.

Hiro lifted his chin, wiped the sneer off his face. "If you'd like your sidekick Veloxity returned to you safely you'll meet my demands." Give it a beat. Two. Time for Captain Champion to stomp around cursing his name a little. "And they are simple. You will meet me at the old quarry outside Smallcity. You will be there at six o'clock, PM. Tomorrow."

Michaela kissed her fingers and waved to him. He bit down on his tongue until the sting chased the urge to smile away. She glowed against the darkness of this bare, efficient room.

"Time for us to see which is better, Captain. My tech? Or your muscles?" He scoffed, making it plain which he thought would conquer. "I dislike being stood up on a date. It makes me testy. And this date is intimate, by appointment only. If you aren't there, if you bring reinforcements, if you involve the authorities or the Legion in any way, you'll never see Veloxity again." *Because I'll have shipped him off to Australia to play with my friend The Bloody Bunyip and he'll be kept too busy to contact you.* "I look forward to seeing you tomorrow."

He pressed the *off* button and the red light stopped blinking. He'd nudged Purriarty out of his lap before he finished standing. He pulled the cape over his head, tossed it on the seat of his chair, and strode towards Michaela.

Her chin went up as she watched him.

"You have an entire room full of your own action figures. An entire room, Hiro. Do you play with them? Got a Legion set for them to fight?" She lifted a hand, pretending to stalk and then pounce on her other hand. "Curse your sudden but inevitable—"

He gripped her hips to pull her close for a hard, hungry kiss. "You're distracting," he growled. "And you made it hard to pet my cat." Closer. He needed her closer. And naked. Yeah. "I don't want to go edit my video and send it. I don't want to prepare for the battle tomorrow. I'd rather be inside you. You're a distraction."

He backed her against the wall behind the camera and dove into the kiss like his life depended on it. The taste of her, the deep, complex flavor. He'd never be able to live without it. "Powers, I love being distracted."

She was here. In his lair. Watching him work with a smile. She knew what would happen, knew she was switching sides. And she'd chosen to do it, to be with him. For *him*.

He angled his head, taking their kiss deeper. The feel of her pressed between him and the wall seduced him. The honeyed, lemon smell of her entrapped him. "Say you know what you're doing, being here with me," he demanded.

"I know what I'm doing." She gripped his hair and kissed him back until his head spun.

"Tell me it's what you want." His mind waited for her to regret her decision and do the smart thing. To leave him. His heart staggered under the magic of her words.

"I want it. I want you."

Why? Why am I worth it? "You have me," he vowed. His voice actually shook. "You'll always have me." *Too much, too fast. Coming in like a creeper.*

Michaela melted against him and gasped, "Hiro...I, I had a question."

"Okay. Anything." He bit down on her lower lip, then soothed the sting with his mouth.

"Why do you hate superheroes so much?"

Ah. That question.

Regretfully, he lifted his head. "Come sit with me." He walked to his villain chair, pulling her with him and fell into its seat. He tugged her onto his lap and kissed her again because he couldn't help it.

She wrapped her arms around him and held on tight. "I'm sorry. I just, feel like I need to know."

In answer, he tugged his Evil Bane cloak out from underneath them. With one swipe, the display attached to the glove lit up. "Can you see this? I know the screen is small."

She leaned closer. "I can see it."

He adjusted her so she was sitting tight against him, back to chest, and peered over her shoulder. It took some digging into buried, encrypted files, but eventually he pulled up the picture he wanted and expanded it to fill the screen.

And his heart shattered all over again.

"It's a family portrait?" She sounded uncertain. She traced the photo frame with a light fingertip as she puzzled it out. "Mom, dad, two kids. The dad...he looks so much like you. Is this your family? Hiro, where are they?"

"Dead."

She slumped against him. "I'm so sorry," she said quietly.

"That's me. My full name, the name my family called me, is Hiroyoshi Saitō." He pointed to the teenager smirking at the side of the photo. How many years had it been since he'd said that name?

"My brother, Yukio. He was ten. In this picture." Briefly, he let his finger brush Yukio's round, happy face.

"My dad, Kobe." Their faces were identical, although Hiro was still ten years away from the age his father had been when he was killed.

"And my mom, Naoko." His hair—the exact same shade and thickness and shine, flowed down her back, around her shoulders. She smiled gently at the camera, her arm around her husband's waist. Hiro had never asked why his father had moved with his new wife from Kobe, all the way across the ocean to Smallcity. Had it been the job? A wish for adventure? Had he been tired of living through yet another massive *Kaiju* battle across the island? He'd never know.

"She's so pretty." Trembling, Michaela nuzzled her head underneath his chin. "The whole family is beautiful. And so happy." She sucked in a breath, hard enough he could feel her chest expanding against his. Then she sighed. "Superheroes killed them?"

He wrapped his arms tighter around her and inhaled her sweet smell. "Supervillains, too. To be fair. They went out for some ice cream after dinner. I was still getting over the stomach flu, so I stayed home. And I lived."

"Oh, Hiro." She pressed his arms closer around her waist. "A battle?"

"Wrecked the freeway," he agreed. "Do you remember that huge invasion about fourteen years ago? You would have been pretty little. But it was a big one, so you might remember. The K'rakk'a came through a portal to take over the world with all those huge monsters.

The Obliterator, Doctor Mamba and Alex Lexor opened the portal. The entire Legion of Superheroes united to wipe them all out and saved the day. Damage was extensive."

"I remember. All those buildings that fell down. Nothing had any Titansteel in it, it hadn't been invented then. I was eight. I stayed home with Mrs. Fish while my parents...they fought in the battle. Oh, Hiro, I'm so very sorry."

"Not your fault. Not my family's. And not mine. They were just on the wrong freeway at the wrong time." He'd never hug his mother again. He'd never speak Japanese with his parents. Or with anyone, really. He'd never listen with Yukio to his father's stories about the beautiful view of Osaka bay from Mount Rokko and how they would visit the city his father was named for someday.

An accident of timing had taken *everything* from him. His parents, his little brother, his home, his history—even his culture and language.

He'd been left with nothing but revenge since then. Revenge, and the burning drive to save as many people as possible. To cover the entire *world* in bubble-wrap so no one else would have to feel as lost as he did.

"So you decided to make sure no one was ever in the wrong place just because they wanted some ice cream, ever again," she said, her voice thick with tears.

"That's about it. Yes."

She twisted her head to touch a soft kiss to his cheek. "And then you became The Evil Bane?"

A laugh tore out of him. It stung his throat. "Actually no. My powers were already pretty clear by then. I worked hard for three years, developing them more. Until I graduated from Secondary School." He didn't like to remember how angry and afraid and lost he'd been all those years. "I invented Titansteel and took it to Technix industries, pretty much demanded they hire me right there. I called myself *Evil's Bane,* then. I was going to keep the whole damn world safe and the first few inventions I made for Technix made that clear."

He closed his eyes and tipped his head to rest against hers. He'd been so sure he was doing the right thing, then. He'd thought he was a hero. "Turns out when you negate their superpowers, the heroes think of you as a villain. They hate feeling powerless." He loved making them feel it. "By the time I was twenty-two I'd bought out Technix, started E.B. Industries, and everyone called me The Evil Bane. I figured, why not? If they're going to call me a villain, I'll *act* like a supervillain."

Michaela was quiet, long enough to make him start worrying. He didn't dare open his eyes. Then, she reached up to cup his jaw with her bare hand.

He was so raw. It felt as if she'd reached inside him and grabbed handfuls of his soul. But it didn't hurt. Didn't pull, or tear, or empty him out. The lonely feeling of a missing family, the rejection of a power no one wanted—she knew them too. He'd felt it, that first time at the pier in Ocean City. They might have started out on opposite sides in this world, but inside they were identical.

Hiro pressed his forehead to Michaela's and held on tight.

Chapter Twenty Four

GENTLY AT FIRST, BUT then firmly, Michaela tugged at Hiro's pain. His loneliness was a bottomless well. An engrained pattern on his heart. Almost too deep-rooted for her to grasp, but nothing resisted an Empath for long.

As she did with Mrs. Fish every few days, as Mrs. Fish did for her, Michaela spun the grief into tiny strands and released it. Gossamer tornadoes in every shade of blue imaginable whirled in her mind. Spinning, twisting, gone into nothing.

Pain could be so beautiful.

It wasn't gone forever. Her power didn't change the structure of the brain, she couldn't replace a pill if medication had been what Hiro needed. And in truth, a loss like his would never really disappear. Michaela's power only let her carry it for a while, give him a short respite from the heavy load. She could soften the ache until there was room to feel something else.

Her fingers tensed against his cheek when she felt the pull. She couldn't stop her own emotions from flowing through their bond. It was the scariest part of her power and—to be strictly honest—the main reason she never touched anyone if she could help it.

No barrier existed to keep the love from seeping out of her, filling the space she'd just emptied. He'd feel it.

As soon as she'd touched him it had been too late to stop.

Please. Please. Don't reject it. Michaela closed her eyes and stopped breathing. *Don't reject me.* Every bit of the new courage she'd grown piled in to keep her hand cupped against his face. Giving her heart—herself—away like this was a terrifying leap into unknown space. All she could do was squeeze her eyes shut and hope he'd catch her.

At first she was sure the love was all her own and she was seconds away from hearing him start laughing at her...but it was Hiro, too.

She felt it, s*aw* it dancing against her closed eyelids like golden mist, trickling inside to fill up *her* empty spaces.

Michaela gasped.

"You can feel it." He sounded satisfied.

"Yes," she whispered. He didn't resent her reaching inside him. Forcing him to take her feelings, too. He was calmer, content, even *happy*. Not pretending, not hiding behind a mask made of sarcasm and careless humor. Really, genuinely happy.

Resting his hand over hers, he pressed her touch more firmly against his cheek.

It was too good to be true. But there was no way to pretend feelings. She'd run into that tactic before, and all she experienced was the badly obvious pretense. So...those really were Hiro's emotions running through her, clear and pure and certain. She couldn't stop smiling and didn't want to.

"Um. I'd like to hear it, too," she said.

His lips curved into the impression of a smile. "I'd like to tell you...that I, I love you, Michaela."

She barely stopped herself from asking *are you sure*? Of course he was sure, she could *feel* it. "Oh, wow. We've only been dating for a few weeks."

"I know." He caressed the back of her hand with gentle fingers, tickling, and the love flowed from him.

Was it greedy of her to drink it in like this? She was *starving* for his affection. "I'm a—I *was* a sidekick. On your opposite side." A reminder for them both.

"I know that, too." He leaned forward to nuzzle her cheek.

She closed her eyes and breathed him in, his closeness, his strength. *Especially* his happiness. Then she raised her other hand so she could cup his handsome face. "My parents are both superheroes. Who you'll have to fight. I might have to help. Pretty soon I'll be facing the Smallcity Chapter to explain myself." Her stomach clenched when he nipped at her chin. Right now, anything Legion seemed faint and far away.

"Yep. It's going to be really damn awkward." He fluttered tiny, sweet kisses against her jaw, the corners of her lips, the curve of her smile. "Is that everything?"

"No. I'm a coward, Hiro. I never stand up for myself. I'm not used to saying what I think or, or fighting for what I want." Even now it was hard to meet his gaze. Her eyes skittered from his to the rest of his face and back. She couldn't stay away from the warmth blazing out of those deep, black eyes for long.

"I don't believe that," he said. "You're speaking up right now. You're no coward, Michaela-chan. You put me in my place all the time. And no spineless jelly could yell at the Fabulous Furia the way you did." A firm, red thread of pride joined the adoration flowing from him.

Powers help her, she lapped that up as eagerly as the love.

"I love you too," she blurted. Her hands froze against the firm line of his jaw. Her heart banged away against her ribs. "I just, none of those problems matters to me when I look at you. It's the wildest thing. I love you so much."

"I can feel it, and it feels beyond wonderful. But it is nice to hear it." He closed his eyes, still smiling. "Really nice."

It was more than nice. It was everything. She'd kept it hidden, locked away, but a part of her had always known *my own parents can't love me, so I must be unlovable. Unworthy*, whispered that piece of her mind. *Wrong. Broken. Worthless. No one wants me.*

Holding onto Hiro like this, she could sense those same thoughts hiding deep inside him. If the smartest, sassiest, most confident supervillain she knew could also fear he was unwanted...then both of them were wrong. Both of them carried the same insecurities. Brought into the open, they shrank from monstrous to tiny. Insignificant.

I'm not wrong. Not broken. I'm powerful. And I'm worth this feeling. Hiro loves me. She relaxed into the certainty. Soaked it up, soft rain into grains of dry sand. *As much I love him.* Sliding her hands to the back of his neck, she wrapped her arms around her heroic supervillain and held on tight. He gripped her back like she was the anchor against his ocean.

"Go finish your video," she said, finally. "The sooner you send it, the sooner you're done for tonight."

Hiro groaned. "I'd rather show you where my bedroom is. Did I show you yet?"

"Yes." She grinned. "I'll check on Veloxity and then I'm going there. I'll wait for you."

"In that case? I'm in a hurry. Give me five minutes."

• • • •

IN THE GIANT MASTER BATHROOM OF HIS PENTHOUSE suite, Michaela finished rinsing with Hiro's mouthwash, and spit into the sink. The charcoal gray, matte-finish bowl of the sink. She eyed the black-tiled walls with her mouth twisted sideways and clicked her tongue against her teeth.

As bathroom colors went, it was like peeing in an underground cavern. She couldn't concentrate on her business when she kept expecting Purriarty to lurch out of a dark corner, muttering about his 'preciouss' and insisting on a game of riddles. She should speak with Hiro about making black the *accent* instead of the main theme.

While she stood considering how to talk him into it, Hiro's arms wrapped around her from behind.

All thoughts of bathroom décor fled into the shadows.

"Hello." He pressed his lips to her shoulder, then wandered his way up to start nibbling on her earlobe.

Warmth spread like a supernova, starting in her shoulder and racing across her body. "Well, hi, handsome." She lifted an arm to wrap around his neck and hold him close. "Did you send your video?"

"Yep. Blasted it to both of his emails, his desktop, and his phone. Who even owns a desktop anymore?"

She laughed. "He's old fashioned. You're lucky he *has* a cell phone. All set to fight him tomorrow?"

"Nope. I'll finish up later."

A quick barb of worry wiggled through her and she turned to face her supervillain. Captain Champion was fast, skilled, and amazingly tough. His age didn't slow him down at all. "Maybe you should go look over your plans, one more time–"

He shifted his hands from her waist to cup her face. "Soon. I will, but I have something more important to do right now."

"Mmm." She closed her eyes and allowed herself to enjoy his touch. "I ought to make you go focus but I like this too much. And I'm sure your plan is a good one." *Pretty sure.*

"I like to think so." Even without looking, she could hear the warm smile in his voice.

Could this get any better? Michaela eased into his hold and tilted her head enough to connect their lips in a light kiss. He was such an amazing kisser. And the things he could do with those clever, slender fingers. She shivered, already anticipating.

As if that wasn't enough, he loved her. Accepted her. Every single piece, even her power. She only hesitated for a second before resting her hand lightly over the back of his. Maybe he'd also like to feel how needy he was making her.

Oh, whoa.

Both of them jolted and it broke their kiss. She cringed, waiting for her hand to be brushed away. His hand slipped, but he didn't break contact with her.

"That's intense," Hiro said, conversationally.

"A little," she agreed. "Is it okay?"

"It's very much okay. It's fucking hot." He shifted and drew her against his chest. He kept his free hand beneath hers, meshed their fingers together, and *squeezed.*

Through every motion the blaze of his arousal pulsed across the link she had opened. It blended and twined with her own, rising higher and higher together.

It was like being dropped off a building into a sheet of crimson flames, soaking in the sweet heat. The air almost shimmered around them.

She hadn't screwed up by touching him. The relief was almost as scorching as his fingers on her.

Michaela spun to face him, causing him to drop their hold. She'd severed the flow of sensation between them, but it didn't matter. For the first time, Michaela could wrap her arms around her lover and *cup the back of his neck with both hands.* Her smile grew, huge and astonished. How many times had she seen a couple do this, as naturally as blinking? How many times had she known there was no way she could do the same?

With her Hiro it was possible. Now she could do anything.

Hiro smoothed his hands up and down her back. Michaela stopped moving anything but her fingers sifting through his soft hair, hoping he'd keep rubbing tingles into her muscles. She nearly arched and purred.

"Have I told you lately I love your Empathy?" he asked. "I can feel everything hiding behind those pretty eyes. You're...blissed out. Like, stuffed full of joy. Relieved. Surprised. Surely thinking some naughty things."

He winked at her. "And...strong? That's not the word. In charge? Triumphant?" He laughed. "Feelings are hard, okay. But don't think I don't notice how turned on you are too."

He leaned closer and brushed their noses together.

Her heart might burst, it was so stuffed full of lovely warm fluff right now. "I'd go with empowered," she told him. "And very turned on. You do that to me." She ran her gaze down his lean body and back up to his soft smile. The view was so perfect she had to hug him tighter. "Hiro, I love you so much."

Now his smile was his Bane-cocky grin. Her whole chest gave another happy squeeze.

She kissed him, nipped him, savored him like a treat. Sank willingly under the desperate ache. It didn't matter that it was close to midnight. Tomorrow meant nothing. Battles were unimportant. The only thing that mattered was getting his hands on her and falling deep into these beautiful feelings together.

With that need driving her, she slid her hands down to grip the edge of his shirt. It buzzed against her fingers, reminding her it was shielded and full of tiny bots that did his bidding. She gripped and pulled it up. *Bye, bots. We're busy now.*

"I like the way you're thinking," he murmured. His fingers traced underneath the edge of her shirt to slide inside the waistband of her jeans.

Air brushed her bared skin softly as he tugged her shirt over her head. E.B. Industries air-conditioning had no chance against the heat they were generating together.

With one hand, Hiro cupped the back of her head and yanked her close for a hard kiss. He wove his fingers through her hair gently even as his mouth devoured hers, fogging her mind with pure lust.

She was fumbling for the button of his pants when the alarms started shrieking.

Chapter Twenty Five

IT TOOK A FEW TOO MANY seconds for the automated scream of Hiro's system alert to make it through to his big brain. With Michaela snuggled up against him, working on unbuttoning his pants, his little brain seemed to have temporarily blocked his ears.

The echoing *boom* which accompanied the floor shivering under his feet—*that* he noticed.

Hiro froze, arms around Michaela, head tilted. *What the fuck?*

Proximity alarms. All of them went off at once and he couldn't pinpoint the origin. *Earthquake? Battle? Captain Champion? No, he doesn't know where my lair is.*

Michaela stepped back, and with a touch of resentment, he released her.

Faint shouting from outside.

The words weren't clear through reinforced walls and Titanglass windows, but he could definitely hear a voice. They were twenty stories up inside his suite and all the alarms were going. He shouldn't have been able to hear *anything*.

"What in the powerless abyss of *hells*?" he wondered aloud.

"I don't know." Michaela rammed her shirt back over her head.

He considered picking up his Bane cloak, but opted to run shirtless for the walnut paneled wardrobe dominating the wall at the foot of his bed. After throwing the doors open, he tugged out the monitor screens. Precious seconds slipped by as he swiped through the menus and brought up his exterior video feeds.

The sudden silence made his ears throb when he dismissed the alarms. But he couldn't see anything on his monitors.

"What were the alarms for?" Michaela asked, leaning around him to look. She sounded calm but her shoulders made a tense curve, poised for battle.

A quick stab of regret caught him right in the guts and he winced. She should be relaxed and enjoying herself in bed right now. With him. Not facing a surprise attack on his lair in the middle of the night.

Maybe Michaela had given up more than he wanted to admit when she walked through the front door of E.B. Industries at his side.

"Intrusion alert. Someone was trying to get into the tower. I don't know...where...yet." He tapped, swiped, tapped. "There. Wait. What?" His cameras were working perfectly, but what they told him was perfectly impossible.

"Here." Michaela's hand flattened against his bare shoulder, and abruptly his confusion was gone, replaced by focus. He felt her own tension, smothered by the determination she was sending him. *I freaking love how she can do that.*

He turned his head to press a quick thank-you kiss to the tips of her fingers.

"Someone tried to enter through the *roof,*" he said. "Does Captain Champion have a hoverboard I don't know about? And how did he find my lair so fast? I sent that video like ten minutes ago."

The roof. All Powers, anything but the roof. He'd been on top of his building—once, and only once—when it was first finished. Even the meter-thick, waist-high parapet he'd ordered built around the entire edge hadn't been enough to get him to step past the threshold of the roof access door. Some deep, instinctive part of him was sure the wind up there would grip him around the ankles with sly, airy fingers, drag him over, and toss him off the edge. Six years later the feeling still left echoes crawling down his spinal column.

He swallowed against the tightening of his throat.

Nope. No, I fucking thank you not. He'd custom-built a bot for the single purpose of installing the security cameras up there and avoided even thinking about it ever since.

"I don't think it's Captain Champion," Michaela said. "Pretty sure it's not."

"Why not?" He narrowed the feeds down to just the upper story and finally had a 360-degree view around his tower. Still nothing. Just a wash of black with pinpricks, rivers, and smears of green night-vision-tinted lights. Smallcity, looking normal at night—

"BANE!"

They both jumped. The cameras had teeny microphone apertures to catch sounds, but that sound hadn't been tiny. No wonder he'd heard it through the walls before the video feeds were open.

"Evil Bane! Release her!" The floor shivered again. Dust sparkled against the black background of the sky in a trailing curtain, past one of the window feeds from the nineteenth floor.

"Oh, fuck, he'll break your whole tower soon," Michaela said in a dismayed whisper.

"What? Who will? Who's *he*?"

Release her the mystery attacker had shouted. *Her*. Not *him*. Not Veloxity. Couldn't have been Captain Champion, then, but who...

"How do we get to the roof?"

Hiro twisted to stare at Michaela in horror. "Why should we go to the roof? I have a jetcar in the basement, we can be there in a few seconds. We'll get out, get clear, regroup. I don't know who's out there, or what they want." Well. He had an idea of what they wanted, but they were never going to get it.

Release her!

He'd lose his powers before he'd send Michaela out to some unknown entity who shouted threats.

None of his camera sensors registered any type of vehicle. Not a helicopter, not a hoverjet, not even an airborne surfboard. His electromagnetic pulse field hadn't been activated. Therefore there were no electronically driven vehicles nearby to cripple with a pulse.

The only possibility left was someone superpowered who could be up twenty stories without support. Someone who could fly.

"No, Hiro, I've got to talk to him. I can get him to stop. He'll break this whole tower down to the foundation before he figures out we're gone. Get me to the roof," she begged.

His mouth dried. He shook his head. "No, no, we'll run, re-group—"

"Please, Hiro. We can't haul Chris all the way down to the basement in time. And we can *not* just leave him here unconscious, he can't even defend himself!"

"I wasn't really going to leave him here defenseless." He might have completely forgotten about the drugged sidekick snoring in his containment room.

"There's a high chance one or all of us will get hurt if we try to run. And your tower. All your hard work. Your experiments. Your *lair*. It will be ruined," she said. "I can fix this. Just get me up there."

A deep voice thundered through the screens. "Bane! Release her, now! She'd better be unharmed." This time he caught the hint of a shape, streaking past a camera.

"We don't have to run. This won't turn into a battle. I can save your lair, all your things here you're still working on. I just need to talk to him," she repeated. Her eyes stayed on his, her gaze steady. She was so calm, and she was asking him to trust her.

Okay. Okay. Get to roof. Stay inside doorway. Shout back at shouting shouter. Come to some sort of verbal arrangement. Never *release Michaela.* A plan to work off, at least. He walked to where his cloak sat crumpled on the floor and snagged it. As he tugged it over his head, he tested the nano-particle shield with an absent tap. It sparked against his finger. Charged and ready to go. Good.

"Okay. Alright. We'll try talking." He gestured towards the doorway. "But if he even *looks* like he's considering attacking, we're getting out of there."

They darted out and into the hallway together, their footsteps pounding in sync. From his peripheral vision Hiro caught a pinkish-gray streak. Purriarty was getting the hells out. He wasn't worried, the cat had hiding places everywhere on their floor. He considered the whole thing his territory. And Purriarty was smart enough *not* to be heading to the *roof.*

Hiro headed to the left down the hallway, breaking into a jog. Michaela rushed to keep up with him. He glanced over as they ran. "Do you know who this is? Tell me what I'm dealing with."

"Pretty sure it's my dad." Michaela almost sounded ashamed.

Hiro missed his next step and came down hard on the opposite foot. He righted himself, gritted his teeth, and moved faster. "Your dad? The one your mom was going to call? The superhero?"

"Yeah. I think she called him."

They reached the stairwell door. Hiro thumbed the lock and it slid open. "How'd he find us? How would he know you were here?"

Their hurried steps echoed off the bare cement walls as they bounded up the stairs. After a few steps, Michaela gasped. "Sharon! I thought I saw Sharon out on the street." She sounded a little breathless, but she kept running at his side. One flight, turn, another flight.

She continued explaining. "When we were coming through the front doors. I just caught a glimpse—the hair," she panted. "Thought it wasn't her, but if it was—and she saw me with you, and called my mom—Hiro, I'm sorry."

He shrugged. "It is—what it is," he puffed. "We just have to calm your dad down." *So, we definitely won't lead off with the fact that we've been seeing each other for weeks. Or that his wife hates me and told me never to see Michaela again. Or that we have lots and lots of the sex.*

As if cued, another shout echoed through the closed door at the top of the stairs. Michaela's dad had a huge, resonant voice. Hiro took a second to pray to any Power listening that the voice didn't correlate to the man's size.

This door required a numeric code, verbal permission, *and* his thumbprint to unlock it. Hiro worked his way through the sequence while his frantic heartbeat ticked away the time. When it clicked open his entire body tensed. A rush of warm, dusty-smelling air blew past them on the stairwell. To Hiro, it smelled like death.

Deliberately, he flexed his fingers to loosen up his hands. "Alright. Okay. Who's your dad? Who are we calming down before he can attack us?" He reached inside his sleeve and fingered different bot options hidden inside. Tranquilizer? Nerve Taze? Bot Net? What would be fast enough to catch a flier?

His legs tried to talk him out of stepping through that open door. Too high. Very much too high.

"UberMeta Man," Michaela said.

She'd stepped past him and was out on the roof before he could unlock his frozen muscles.

"What?" he asked the empty black doorway, dazed.

Finally he forced his legs to cooperate. One step, then two, and that was all he could push himself to do. Michaela was already near the center of the roof, head craned so she could survey the dark sky. She turned slowly, pivoting on one heel. Her hair fluttered in the ever-present wind, as dark as the sky spread over them.

"*What*?" he said, louder.

The edge of the roof loomed bigger and bigger in his vision. A chasm large enough to swallow the entire world, creeping closer and closer. He locked up, unable to move any more, but even the void couldn't distract him completely from the bombshell she'd just lobbed. "Your *dad* is *UberMeta Man*?" he hissed at Michaela. "Are you *serious*?"

From far, far below he could hear faint banging. Then a metallic, muffled crunching noise. Inside, the alarms started hooting again.

She nodded, looking distracted. "I don't see him. I think he's down there breaking things to get in." Frustration dropped spikes in her tone.

"No one ever sees him! You don't see UberMeta Man coming! He just super-speeds past and kicks everyone's ass. Ever powerful damn it,

Michaela. I can't do this. Come back here. It's so high." His voice shook. He was too terrified to care.

Immediately she turned and walked back to him, hand outstretched. "I forgot. Here."

He gripped her extended fingers, tugged her closer, and soaked up the calm she was offering. While she was tucked against his chest he took the chance to kiss her because he might not have the opportunity again for a while.

After she'd held onto him for a few seconds, absorbing his panic, he cooled enough to focus on the security systems on his wrist screen. "Thanks," he told her. "Much better." Again, he had to wonder how she could possibly be so calm in this kind of situation. Maybe having *UberMeta Man* as your *dad* gave you a high tolerance for emergencies.

He had to let go of her hand so he could tap through and dismiss the alarms again. Instantly, he missed her strengthening presence in his mind. "Looks like he tried to force the back doors." He pursed his lips, slightly impressed. "It looks like the Titanglass is holding, against UberMeta Man. Unexpected, but wow."

"Michaela...coming in! You'll...alright." More shouting, a bit muffled, floated up from below. UberMeta Man's promise was followed by more crashing sounds.

Hiro winced. "Can you maybe start yelling for him? Get him up here?" He'd probably attack on sight. Hiro tried to flick through his mental options. Pretty much every single one ended with him grabbing Michaela and ducking, dodging, or hiding. He was so not prepared to take on the strongest superhero in the entire universe. He'd planned on another few years before he even thought about *trying*.

"I've got a way to get him up here, quickly. And it'll make him stop breaking things. Trust me, okay?" Michaela said.

Something rolling under the surface of her voice made Hiro look up from his screen. "I do, I always–Michaela? Where are you going?" He grabbed for her, but she stepped smoothly out of reach.

"Trust me," she said again. She looked at him over her shoulder, and the ambient glow from the tower floodlights behind them touched her smile. She turned and continued walking.

"I trust you completely, but, ah, wait, you're a little close to the edge there. Michaela." His voice rose higher, sharper with every word. She didn't stop.

His fingers ached where they were wrapped around the metal doorframe. Every cell in his body screamed at him. She was too close to the blank, hungry nothing which went down twenty stories. Too close, and he couldn't force his legs to follow.

"Michaela." Caught in some sort of horrifying dream, Hiro watched her grab the parapet. "Michaela, *no*!" He tried to shove his legs forward, but his body tried to hold him back. The conflicting urges knocked him to his knees. "Michaela you can shout from over here. Come back." He reached out for her with both arms, grasping with his power to bring her back to his side.

"UberMeta Man! *Get the fuck up here*!" he shouted desperately. It was like trying to grip a breeze. His potenkinesis wasn't strong enough to lift a whole person. His head pounded as he threw everything he had into his power, and it still wasn't enough.

"I've got this. It's okay," she said. "I inherited one other power you didn't know I have, from my dad." Standing on the parapet, she turned to fully face him.

"It had fucking better be *flight*!" A hellish glow from the floodlights outlined the entire rooftop, sharpening every awful detail. The electric life pulsing through Smallcity reflected off a thin cloud cover.

Michaela's feet were centimeters from the edge.

The taste of hot metal burned in his mouth. "No. Please, just, come back."

"I'm invulnerable, I got it from him. It's going to be fine, Hiro. See you in a second." Her smile was calm and unafraid, so sweet; and he would never, ever forget how it felt to watch that smile disappear when she leaned backward gracefully and let gravity eat her.

Chapter Twenty Six

WIND SCREAMED IN MICHAELA'S ears as she plummeted towards the earth. "UberMeta Man!" she shouted. "I need help!"

Anyone could shout that phrase at any time, in any universe, and UberMeta Man would hear it. As soon as he could respond, he'd be there.

All her life she'd watched him zoom away to help someone else who had called on him. Well, now it was time for him to come to her rescue.

With him already here, trying to crack open Hiro's lair and peel her out like a nut, it should be less than a few seconds. For his daughter, she hoped, even faster. She crossed her arms over her chest and closed her eyes, waiting. Air squeezed around her like a too-tight, tearing glove.

Anticipating.

Still waiting.

Hiro was probably hardcore freaking out back up on the roof. *Trust me, lover. Please don't be too scared.* If she'd had time, she would have explained more. She should have told him before it came to a test. But this particular power was her last stand, her only-for-dire-emergencies secret.

A secret ingrained so deeply she couldn't even *think* about speaking it out loud.

Just like her Empathy. Just like her real feelings about superheroes and the Legion. And the battle casualties she treated every day at work.

There were a lot of things she hadn't allowed herself to say or even wonder about. Secrets had always surrounded her, securing her like fortress walls, and it hadn't occurred to her that even though they kept her safe, they also kept her locked away.

That was all going to change, starting tonight. She'd damn well say exactly whatever she wanted to whoever she wanted, from now on. No walls. No more biting her tongue to force the words back when she had better reasons to let them free.

Although she fell, somehow the air still pushed down on her, a punishing mass. The pressure would make her black out if she didn't get some relief soon. She tightened every muscle in her body, focusing on staying aware. *Any second now, dad!*

"UberMeta Man! I need help, *now*." This time, real urgency coated her tone. She hoped her father heard it.

When she wedged one eye open, she saw a smear made of lights speeding past, which only made her dizzier. She closed her eye again. Her fingers and toes tingled as if she'd plunged them into an ice bath. She recognized the signs of her body slipping into fight-or-flight, protect-vital-organs mode.

She'd told Hiro why this wouldn't kill her, even if her father didn't save her, but she hadn't given him enough time to really *believe* her. When she returned to his side she'd explain. In full detail.

And while the landing wouldn't kill her it would hurt enough that she might wish it had. She'd never been able to manage a proper superhero landing.

Arms like steel bands caught her under the shoulders and at the back of her knees, jerking her body to an abrupt halt. Breath exploded out of her in a huge *whoof*. Her head whipped back on her neck, and she caught a trace of the scent of distant stars.

She risked a tentative peek. "Hi, Dad."

"What were you *thinking*?" Her father's mouth was tight and grim. All the muscles on his face seemed set in stone. Even the dense curls of his hair looked tense. "Don't answer that. Was leaping off the roof the only option you had to escape?"

"No, wait no, no escaping. I wasn't escaping. I need you to take me back." The edge of E.B. Industries loomed above them. She'd fallen about halfway down the building before he caught her. "Take me back, please." She pointed up.

"No. The Evil Bane or one of his minions was holding you hostage. I'm getting you out of here, Michaela." He held her tighter against his broad chest as he zoomed down the nearest street, still ten stories above the cars lighting up the night below. "And I *really* wish there had been another, less dangerous way for you to escape."

"No, I wasn't a hostage. No danger. Sharon had her facts wrong." It had to have been Sharon who set all this in motion. The only other person who had seen her with Bane that day was snoring in the containment room back at E.B. Industries. "Dad, take me back. I-Ivan, my, um, boyfriend, is going to be really scared right now. I need to let him know I'm fine." She'd almost forgotten to call Hiro by his alter-identity, which would have been the crowning blunder in a night full of errors.

"Michaela..." her father inhaled and released a breath slowly through his nose, clearly grappling for patience. "Sharon *saw* this Ivan person grab you and drag you inside. He had someone else draped over his shoulder. The Evil Bane is obviously making a big play on several superheroes at once by kidnapping their sidekicks and, sweetest heart, I hate to tell you this but...Ivan is his minion."

Well, shit. Not quite. But put that way, it did look bad. "He's not—well he kind of is a minion—okay it's not really like that. There's no kidnapping plot. I can explain everything." She couldn't explain in any way he'd accept that she had just helped capture Veloxity and there was, in fact, a kidnapping plot.

Oh, Sweet Supers, everything was such a mess. Briefly, Michaela squeezed her eyes shut in a wince. This would make shouting at her mother in the middle of a crowded restaurant look like a comfortable family game night with hot cocoa.

"It's not what it looked like," she tried again. "I walked in there of my own free will, and we need to turn around now." Michaela twisted so she could peer over his broad shoulder. As they zoomed away the red letters which spelled out E.B. were shrinking to dots in the distance. Somewhere up there Hiro was scared for her. She had to go back. She had to fix this. "Dad, go back, now!"

He shook his head and kept flying.

It was as if a tether hooked firmly to her heart was stretching, stretching, about to snap.

"*Dad*," she said, warningly. "Do *not* make me feed you what I'm feeling right now." Michaela raised one bare hand. In the dim city glow she saw him flinch and, through everything else going on, that flinch still hurt.

"Michaela it's not *safe*. How do I know he won't keep you there, to get at me? He's a *minion*."

"You have to trust me. There is no plot involving you, and Ivan is not a threat to us." She spread her fingers wide, making it obvious, and reached for his bare neck. If she had to she'd force this *need* to get back to Hiro on her dad. Fill him up with panicked urgency until he flew her where she wanted to go. She *hated* to force her feelings on people and had never done it on purpose in her life. But for Hiro, she would.

Before her fingers touched her father's skin he let out a frustrated noise, a bit like a growl. Hair puffed into her face as they turned, and Michaela lowered her hand. She shoved her hair away and let herself grin. "Right up to the roof. I'll introduce you to Ivan. We have lots to talk about."

"Mmph," he grunted, sounding much less than enthusiastic.

"Do not shoot your eye lasers at him," she commanded.

Her father grumbled a noncommittal noise.

"I'm serious. No lasers. No super breath. *No* fighting. Give me a chance to explain everything," she insisted.

"Mmph."

She tucked her smile away and folded her hands in front of her. Buildings whipped past below them. E.B. Industries looked like a sped-up frame from a movie, getting larger in fast forward. Her heart had barely started slowing from its frantic pace. Surely her father would understand, once he met Hiro as 'Ivan'. Once he saw how happy Hiro made her and she explained more of what had happened to them.

He would accept everything she'd had to do. Wouldn't he?

Chapter Twenty Seven

THEY TOUCHED DOWN AT the center of the roof of E.B Industries, several meters away from the access door. Michaela immediately found Hiro sitting just inside the doorway, hands wrapped around his bent knees.

"Michaela!" Hiro shot up so fast he stumbled on the first step. He rushed over to where UberMeta Man stood with her in his arms.

She started wiggling, trying to get down.

Her father tightened his arms around her.

"Michaela." Hiro reached inside the superhero's caging arms and ran his hands over her hair and face. He traced the slope of her shoulders, down to her wrists and fingers. Even his potenkinesis brushed over her in fast sweeps, touching everywhere his hands weren't. His touches communicated such intense urgency, her stomach started fluttering.

"Michaela. Okay. Okay. You're okay." He skipped his hands around UberMeta Man like the large man didn't exist and pressed lightly on her side, then checked over her knees, down to her feet. He pushed away the hem of her leggings to circle her ankles with his fingers, testing the bones.

Then he tugged off her shoes so he could bend every one of her toes. Apparently satisfied, he let out a relieved sounding breath and ran a hand through his tousled hair. "Oh, fuck, okay. You're fine."

"I said I would be. I'm really sorry," she said. Her eyes itched. She sternly instructed herself not to cry, as Hiro replaced her shoes with as much care as if they'd been spun glass.

Disregarding the fact that she was still being cradled by a superhero wearing his irritated face, Hiro leaned forward to frantically kiss her face, her lips, her hair. "Let's never do that again ever. Promise? Nothing even *approaching* anything in a vaguely similar realm as jumping off a roof." He cupped her face and kissed her once more. "No jumping at the pool. No jumping off stairs. Not even off a curb, ever again, okay?"

"Stop," she chuckled, and then sniffed. "You're just getting silly now. I promise not to jump off any other roofs." The chances of this exact set of coincidences stacking up again were tiny enough. "Never again."

UberMeta Man took two steps back and swung her protectively to the side, making Hiro's hands slip from her face. "Does either one of you want to explain what's going on? And you'd better quit kissing my d—Michaela."

Michaela twisted in his arms. "Would you put me down?"

"No." The word landed like an anvil.

She sighed. "Fine. UberMeta Man, this is Ivan O'Reilly. Ivan, this is UberMeta Man." She and Hiro both knew this was her dad, but it might make her dad happier if *he* thought that was still a secret.

Her father's jaw popped, a warning sign, and he took another step backward. Okay, the carefully worded introduction hadn't worked.

"Michaela, I don't like any of this," her father said urgently. "It all smells like a trick. The Evil Bane could be hiding anywhere. You're not safe here." His tone indicated he was one wrong look away from flying away with her.

Hiro threw out both hands, palms up and flat. "Please. Please stay. No trick. The Evil Bane is not going to attack you. Hi. I'm Ivan. I'm a reporter for Smallcity Broadcasting. It's nice to meet you, sir."

"The Evil Bane's minion is a reporter?"

"Freelance," Michaela said. "And there's so much you don't know about what he does. He's saved a lot of people. We're not tricking you. He's not after you. I promise."

"Then why are you here?" His voice echoed exhaustion, but he stood tall and carried her weight as if it he didn't notice it. Everyone knew UberMeta Man could handle anything, and Michaela knew it, too.

Impulsively, Michaela wrapped her arm around her father's neck to hug him. She kept her hands away from his skin. He'd had enough to deal with already tonight. "This is so hard for you. Isn't it."

"It's obvious there's a lot going on that I don't know about." He squeezed her tight for a brief moment, and then let go. Her feet touched the rooftop and she wobbled straight. She looked up into her father's familiar stern expression and smiled.

As soon as she was within grabbing distance Hiro took her by the waist and pulled her to him. He buried his face in her neck and held on tight.

"It's okay. I'm okay."

"I know." His voice was muffled against her skin. His breath fanned warmly against her throat. "I just need to hold on to you for one second to make sure."

Her eyes stung again and she blinked, hard. "I'm really sorry. Again. Sorry."

Finally he pulled back, but only far enough to cup her face in his hands and give her a fierce kiss.

Off to the side, UberMeta Man cleared his throat with a loud, annoyed rumble.

As they broke apart, Michaela let out a strained laugh. "I can explain." She kept her arms around Hiro's neck, and he fastened his around her waist in a tight grip.

"I'm getting the basic idea," her father said, wryly. "But I'd appreciate a few more details. And I need to call the Fabulous Furia off."

"What?" Michaela stiffened.

He nodded. One side of his mouth twitched, the faintest hint of a smile. "She's waiting twelve blocks over to guard our escape from The Evil Bane. To be honest, I think she's *itching* to get at him. We were going to escort you to the safe house tonight." He reached for the gold armband high up on his left bicep.

Everyone always thought the bands covered another huge muscle or were there to make a nice contrast with his royal blue suit, but both of them bulged because he kept things hidden there. Like gel protein packs, and his phone.

"Oh," she said, weakly. Hiro patted her back and she leaned into him. "Can we, um, do this without her here? Just for now?" One parent at a time would be hard enough.

"I'll call her and tell her you're fine. You two"—one thick, blunt finger stabbed at each of them— "stay right there. Don't move."

"Not a centimeter," Hiro assured him.

UberMeta Man gave him a deeply suspicious look as he unlocked his phone.

Chapter Twenty Eight

HIRO SIGHED AND WRAPPED his arm more firmly around Michaela. He couldn't really think of a way this discussion could go worse. Perhaps if another portal opened, right on the roof, and Mucosa monsters from the Slime Dimension started popping out. Or a lighting storm blew in, with them trapped twenty stories up on the roof. Or both at the same time.

Electrified, sentient snot attack would be worse than this, objectively.

But not much worse.

"No. No. You can't just turn your back on everything you've fought for your whole life," UberMeta Man said, again, waving his massive arms for emphasis. His tone tensed more with each repetition. He paced back and forth across the roof in front of them.

Michaela had briefly and clearly explained to her father that she hadn't listened to Furia's command to have nothing to do with Ivan O'Reilly. That in fact, she loved him, and she wasn't giving him up even though he worked for The Evil Bane. As her father gaped at her, she'd outlined the things Bane and E.B. Industries had created which saved millions of lives. And she'd dropped the bomb that she thought those things were necessary. So necessary, she was changing sides to help Ivan as a minion.

That was a lot of explosions for one conversation and the results were, accordingly, a fiery hot mess.

Hiro was so proud of her he thought he might burst from it. Her father looked ready to just plain burst. Hiro had never seen the superhero near her before but now, knowing their relationship, he could pick out the little things she'd inherited from him. The arch of her brows, the thick, dark hair. Even her eyes were the same color and shape. Her skin was a lighter sand tone than his earth brown. She was such a fascinating mix of her father and mother. Hiro could easily see them both in the structure of her face.

Where her Empathy came from, however, was probably a mystery to all of them.

"I'm not turning my back on anything. I'll still be helping people, maybe even helping them *more*." She waved a hand in-between them, scrubbing with frustrated speed. "And let's not pretend I was actually fighting for goodness or right or anything. I barely assisted in a tiny fraction of Furia's battles before I gave being a sidekick up for nursing school. You can't tell me the entire Legion thought I was anything other than a token low-power." Grief boiled and seethed in her voice.

Hiro reached out with his free hand to grasp her fingers and pull her hand to his lips. If it were possible, he'd spare her this entire conversation, all of the old hurt it was dragging up and the new tears it was ripping in her heart. Through their linked fingers, the fresh, gaping wounds inside her washed over him and nearly knocked him to his knees. Again, the strength inside her amazed him.

This wasn't easy for Michaela. He tenderly kissed her knuckles again and sent her as much of his pride as he could.

When he looked up, he caught UberMeta Man staring at their hands, at the kiss Hiro was pressing to her skin, looking uncomfortable.

No one likes what I can do Michaela had told him at the pier, and her open pain said she knew it well. How much of that knowledge was due to her own parents? Her father? He for damn sure didn't look like he shared his feelings with her on a regular basis. The invincible hero actually seemed afraid of what she could do.

Looking UberMeta Man right in the eyes, Hiro said to Michaela, "You're not just a token. Your power can do nearly anything. Maybe they were afraid to use it."

Outlined in the floodlights, the dashing superhero shook his head jerkily. "That's not it, and it's not relevant. You can't possibly want to be a *minion*, Michaela." His voice sounded ragged. "You'd have to choose evil, every day. You'd fight against your friends. The Legion. Against," he swallowed, "*Furia* and me." He darted his gaze to Hiro, then back to his daughter.

Trying to even speak around the *edge* of this secretive family's mysteries was like yanking teeth.

Fresh pain surged through Michaela and into him. Hiro braced against it and held her tighter as she replied, "I'm hoping I wouldn't have to fight at all. I never really liked the fighting anyway. I just...want to help. It's all I've ever wanted. I want to save people."

"A supervillain will never save people. You're dreaming, honey. What's it going to take for you to wake up?"

"A supervillain has *already* saved lives. Why can't you just admit that?" Michaela asked. Her voice caught and tears tracked down her cheeks, shining in the rooftop glow.

"Stop it," Hiro said, harshly. "Fucking stop. Can't you tell how much you're hurting her with this?"

UberMeta Man stepped forward, reaching out as if he'd love nothing better than to yank Michaela away. "There's no need to curse at me. You and your employer are *no good for her*. You should have listened to her mother and stayed away from her."

"He is nothing *but* good for me," Michaela argued back.

Her body jerked in Hiro's arms, twisting to look around her father, at the empty night sky.

The next thing he knew, he was flat on his back. Somehow, she'd shoved and tripped him at the same time, taking them both into a controlled fall. All that fight training she'd had as a sidekick.

She threw her body over his, spreading her arms wide.

He'd just opened his mouth to ask her why when the world caught fire.

Something heavy landed on his legs, crushing them into the roof. Michaela screamed, but she sounded more angry than afraid. He couldn't organize his brain enough to understand what she'd said. Not when vivid shades of orange and red and gold filled his vision. Not when wild roaring stopped his ears, and everything around him seared with heat. The nanobots shielding them sizzled and popped, but luckily held their barrier.

The blazing heat stopped. All noise stopped. Everything stopped and the sudden silence rang as loud as the roaring had. Wisps and tendrils of smoke swirled up from the metal around them. The smell of hot rocks, or maybe burnt dust, floated over them.

He tried moving and realized that roughly 270 pounds of UberMeta Man muscle lay over his legs. That was the reason they were squashed. He jerked up his knee, as a hint, and the superhero stood slowly.

Michaela bounded off his chest and squared up to face the Fabulous Furia. "What the powerless *fuck* was that, Furia!"

Hiro seconded that question even as he wondered, a little groggily, where timid Michaela had gone off to. He couldn't quite process that Furia had just tried to kill him on the roof of his own lair. Obviously, he should have left his perimeter and EMPs active but he'd wanted UberMeta Man to know he was talking peacefully, not priming for battle.

His move towards good faith had come back to burn him right in the ass. The lack of protection had allowed Furia to storm the rooftop on a hoverbike and join the party.

He stood cautiously, fighting the urge to check his hair for singeing. He was fairly sure Michaela's mom had crisped some of it off. Michaela reached out and grabbed his hand tightly enough to leave dents in his skin.

They faced off, the sidekick and the supervillain against her superpowered parents.

Furia planted her feet like a warrior queen and tossed her hair back. "I told you not to have anything to do with him. I told you I would call your father. I hate to say it, Michaela, but I told you so."

Chapter Twenty Nine

RED HOT ANGER ROARED through Michaela's chest, sweeping away any trace of her usual timid demeanor. Furia had crossed every line imaginable tonight and Michaela *would not* let her get away with it.

"Guess what?" she shot at Furia. She let go of Hiro's hand so she could throw both arms out in a wide, sarcastic sweep. "*I didn't listen.* And I will not listen. You may *not* try to roast my boyfriend in front of me. Ever. That is not okay."

"Boyfriend?" Furia repeated, scowling furiously.

"Boyfriend," Michaela affirmed. "*Roasting: no.* Not okay. Also, I'm switching to his side. I'm not asking for permission, I am telling you. Try to set the Legion on me. Just try it, and I'll tell them, too."

Furia's hands started to glow like banked embers—as good as a warning siren. Next would come another shot at Hiro.

Something built inside Michaela, ready to burst. Something fierce and full and *huge*, boiling like a thunderstorm on the horizon. A tiny part of her was grateful she wasn't touching Hiro and he wouldn't have to feel this twisted, ugly knot inside her. This tangle of emotions had been growing and growing all her life, hidden in her depths, tied down by secrets.

Those ties were breaking so fast she could almost hear the snaps. She could feel the echo of them lashing through the air as she let everything fly.

"Okay. Alright. Truth time, you guys." She took a deep, gasping breath and went on, "I have always hated the battles, okay? I have always been in the background, useless, ignored, left behind. My weak power has always been against me and I *hate* it."

Furia croaked a protest. "Mic—"

Michaela whipped her chin up to pin her mother with a look. "No. My turn. You and dad, you made me feel *worthless*. I wasn't a good sidekick. I'm not a good daughter. Out of all the incredible powers I could have inherited, I didn't get the right ones. I barely made it as a sidekick and we *all* know I only got in because dad is so powerful the Legion didn't dare say no." She choked out a harsh laugh. Her parents looked so horrified, hearing that truth. "Dad says I'm dreaming, but it's so much better than being wide awake while your *own parents* are afraid to touch you, while they're rushing around saving everyone else in the entire fucking world and ignoring the shit out of you."

"Michaela don't swear," UberMeta Man replied, on automatic. "I–I didn't...I didn't ever mean to ignore you. I've *never* thought of you as a token member of anything." His whole face softened and he rubbed the back of his neck. "That's not what I meant to give the impression of. We *love* you. I love you."

"Not enough," Michaela said bitterly. "Not enough to accept me." She caught her mother's wince, viciously glad to see it. "Not enough to be there for me." That shot she directed at her father, although her heart twinged to do it. "Do you know how many stupid battles Furia set me up on, hoping I'd prove how badass I was to Smallcity? Do you know how many other heroes tried to step in front of me when she did—like I was this powerless, helpless problem for her to solve?"

She hadn't realized she was crying again until Hiro brushed a kiss at the corner of her eye and his kiss left a cool, wet tingle on her skin. His presence at her side steadied her, although she kept her hands to herself. She'd needed to bring these secrets out into open air for a *long* time. And she had to do this on her own.

Any hint of glow had faded from Furia's palms now. She looked stunned. "No, Michaela, that's not how I see you. You've never been a problem, or helpless, to me."

"Coulda fooled me," Michaela said. "No one is...as deeply rooted in me as you and dad, so no one else has the power to hurt me like you can. And you've hurt me plenty," she told them, softer now.

"I never wanted to. I had no idea, Michaela," her father sounded gutted.

"I know. I didn't tell you. We're so good at keeping secrets in our family. Aren't we. But now I'm telling you. I'm saying what I feel. Do you know why, after all these years?"

Mutely, he shook his head. Furia shrank back a step, huddling into her husband's side.

Michaela tilted her head to indicate Hiro. "Because he's standing here next to me and giving me some of his strength. Because he loves me." She squared her shoulders defiantly. "He loves every *part* of me. He's everything you both never gave me, and I'm not changing my mind. I picked this man. I picked his side. I need you, for once, to support this. Even though it comes with some changes you don't like. Please. Do this for me. You can never accept my power if you want but please, just give me this."

The ever present wind whistled emptily around their odd group, superheroes, sidekick, and villain. Somewhere far below, bass throbbed through a car's speakers like a muffled heartbeat.

"I don't know if I can," UberMeta Man said slowly. "I'll never be on the side of evil and I don't want you to be. But," he uncrossed his arms, "I can try to accept your choice of boyfriend, at least. I do love you, Michaela. I'm sorry if I—if it seemed like I don't. I just—I guess I figured that you knew."

One parent down. Michaela turned to look at Furia and her relief splintered into shock.

Thin, wavering blue lines trickled down Furia's face. They dripped off her chin, danced through the air to land on the roof with tiny *hisses*.

The superhero was crying flames.

UberMeta Man wrapped his arm around his wife's shoulders and tugged her close. He nuzzled the top of her head, murmuring something Michaela couldn't catch. He didn't look surprised to see his wife crying drops of fire, only heartbroken.

"You were such a good baby." Furia wiped away an azure tear, looking at Michaela.

"What? What does that have to do with anything?" Michaela asked. She'd meant to get everything out in the open but she wasn't prepared to see her mother cry.

"We're all telling our truths now," Furia said. "And, truthfully, you were the sweetest baby. It was such a miracle that I got pregnant at all, and then I had you and it was—we were so—" she made a helpless gesture.

The more powerful the superhero, the less fertile that superhero was. It appeared to be nature's way of making sure the Empowered didn't take over the earth. And Samuel Elias Martin—UberMeta Man—was one of the most powerful beings the world had ever seen. Michaela really had been an unexpected marvel.

Furia continued, "I loved letting you hold onto my fingers while you nursed. You had nothing but happy feelings to send me." She swiped impatiently at her cheeks but the flames kept dripping. "And then when you were ten months old you caught some sort of virus while you were teething. You had a fever; you wouldn't keep anything down, just kept throwing everything up. We were both miserable and you cried and screamed and cried. I felt like I was going to lose my mind. We'd been up all night and most of the next day and you just wouldn't stop crying and then you—your little hand landed on my arm and—"

"Oh, mom," Michaela whispered.

"It wasn't your fault but I was so exhausted and impatient and so *angry*. You sensed all of it. I *scared* you. I felt how scared you were. My perfect, miracle baby girl and you were afraid of me. I had to put you down alone in your crib and leave the room. I felt like the worst mother in every galaxy."

"But...but that was years ago. Why are you still—why will you still not touch my bare hand?" Michaela asked. Empathy was supposed to make her the expert on emotions. Why had she never guessed that Furia's aversion came from fear?

"After that, every time I tried I was terrified I'd hurt you again. I couldn't even contemplate being angry or impatient and having you feel it and I just...it turned into a bit of a phobia, I guess." Furia closed her eyes, her mouth trembling.

"I didn't want to make your mother feel worse, so I avoided touching your hands, too," UberMeta Man admitted. "I also have a lot of emotions that—especially after a battle there are things I don't *want* you to have to feel. But I wasn't rejecting your power. We weren't. I didn't mean to make it seem like that."

"Well, I kind of was rejecting it," Furia said. "I haven't been comfortable with your power since you were a baby, but I love you, Michaela. I do just want you to feel normal but only because that seemed *safe* to me. I want you to be safe, and happy, more than anything. And this boy" —she gestured at Hiro, then swiped away tears again— "is not safe. Being a minion is not safe. I won't let you do it."

Michaela gathered up everything squirming around in her stomach. All the pain and relief and irritation and rage and what felt like a *hundred* other emotions, fighting and writhing for space. She took a deep breath and let a whisper of it escape. A psychedelic rainbow of colors swirled from her chest over their small group.

Furia's admission changed the way Michaela saw her. A fundamental, deep change, which she hoped would, maybe, help her find a little more closeness with her mother. But it didn't change the fact that Michaela had spent years being rejected and left out by both parents. For the sin of being born with her powers. It didn't change all the times Furia had refused to accept Michaela's uncomfortable reality, instead of being an ally for her daughter. Furia had been afraid, but that didn't give her the right to push Michaela away or dismiss her problems.

And it didn't change the fact that, fourteen years ago, her parents had fought in the battle which ripped Hiro's entire family from him.

Even worse, if Michaela explained the consequences of that battle and pointed out what they had been complicit in, Furia still wouldn't see why it was such a terrible thing. UberMeta Man might, but Furia never would. She just...wouldn't get it.

Standing alone with her fists clenched at her sides, Michaela fought to settle what she'd thought she knew with what she understood, what she felt with what she wanted. Most of all, right now, she wanted it understood that her parents had no say in *letting* her do anything.

Once her swirling emotions had calmed a little, she heaved a sigh and looked firmly at her parents. "First, mom, I'm giving you a hug. No arguing."

"I wasn't going to," Furia said, and opened her arms.

Chapter Thirty

HIRO HAD TO FORCE HIMSELF not to reach out and pull Michaela back to his side as she went to hug her mother and father. Part of him didn't trust the superheroes and expected them to keep hurting Michaela.

He wanted to believe they'd reached some sort of healing point, for her sake, but he didn't think her father would ever get over her switching to the side of Evil. Not really.

And her mother would never believe Michaela was safe when she was fighting alongside a supervillain. She'd continue trying to separate Michaela from him. He'd never met another superhero so stubbornly set in her ways. All Powers, she'd probably try to roast him extra crispy every time he turned his back on her.

Flexing his stiff fingers, Hiro watched UberMeta Man wrap his brawny arms around both wife and daughter. He lowered his head to rest it on Furia's curls. It was a good thing the family shared invulnerability, with Furia's fiery tears landing everywhere.

There had to be a way Michaela could be with him, work at his side, and still be accepted by her parents. He wasn't going to be the cause of more pain for her, more tears, not after what she'd already dealt with. The deepest center of him rebelled utterly against causing her that kind of damage. After all, *he* wasn't her parents.

If he could just think of something. The answer must be right there. He only had to find it.

When their family hug had tapered down to sniffles and hiccups, Hiro stepped forward. "You know, it occurs to me that The Evil Bane might be focusing too hard on only one side of the fight."

All of them stared at him. It struck him, hard, how much he wished he could hold onto his family like that. He wouldn't take that away from Michaela.

"What?" Michaela swiped the back of her hand over her eyes and sniffed.

"I think he's focused too hard on superheroes," Hiro explained. "At the core of it, he's always been trying to protect the regular, everyday unpowered. From *any* threat, no matter where it's coming from. Maybe it's time for him to start inventing things that cancel out some supervillain powers."

A tentative smile bloomed on Michaela's face. She must have already guessed where he was going with this.

UberMeta Man only seemed confused. "You would ask your villain to...switch sides? Start working for the Legion of Heroes? I don't think that can ever happen."

Hiro pressed his lips together and fought down a snort. *Superheroes. It's always a half empty glass with them.* "No, not switching sides. No one, including The Evil Bane, would trust him in the Legion. I'm thinking more a solo act."

"He'd be a vigilante," Michaela said, with a touch of pride. "Saving wherever he was needed."

UberMeta Man raised one massive hand to pinch the bridge of his nose. "Fantastic. *Two* different sets of supers after him. Even *more* dangerous for you, Michaela."

"Too dangerous," Furia put in. She sounded much less broken than she had a few minutes ago.

"Risky, maybe, but not evil. She wouldn't be a minion. She'd be assisting a rogue billionaire vigilante as he fights crime and protects citizens outside the limits of the law," Hiro said.

Michaela made a face. *Billionaire?* she mouthed at him, her nose scrunched up.

Hiro winked.

"And The Evil Bane would listen to you? You have that much influence?" UberMeta Man said in disbelief.

Now Michaela's face was a picture titled *acute irony*.

"Yes."

"Well, I'll believe it when I actually see it."

"I create all of his inventions. Everything. Sir." Hiro rocked back on his heels, hid his smirk, and enjoyed the shockwaves coming off of that one. "Freelance reporting is more of a hobby. I'm mostly an inventor."

"...I see." UberMeta Man looked from his daughter to Hiro. "And this is what you want? What you're choosing?"

"Yes," she said.

The most beautiful word he'd ever heard. It filled Hiro with a fizzing, sparkly kind of warmth he'd never felt before. Again, she chose him. For the first time in an awfully long time he could see a clear future. A good, busy, full, complicated future. And she stood next to him in every single vision.

"Michaela think about this for a second," Furia said. "A vigilante? How would that be a good idea for you?"

Michaela gave her mom a quick squeeze, then returned to Hiro's side. "I'm an adult, mom. And I can make choices like this. You don't have to like them, but I will ask you to step back and let me make them."

"You're definitely mature enough to speak your mind," her mother replied tartly.

"Yes. Yet another benefit from hanging around with my vigilante boyfriend. And that's not going to change," Michaela warned.

Hiro held out a hand and she took it. A complex, tangled weave of her emotions washed over him, but the brightest thread in it was joy. He'd do anything, steal or fix or create anything, even take on the whole superpowered world, to keep that happiness the first thing she felt every day.

Although, speaking of fixing and creating...he eyed UberMeta Man speculatively. The superhero stood like an unalterable monolith, massive biceps crossed in front of his chest, dark eyes centered on his daughter. Didn't he have laser vision? Hiro was nearly sure he'd heard it was one of UberMeta Man's many, many powers.

Maybe the superhero would help him test out the glass which had been giving him so much trouble. His left arm twinged at the memory.

Michaela had caught him watching UberMeta Man, and felt the flex of his arm at her side. Of course she put it together. One of the many reasons he adored her was for her intelligence. She shook her head at him. "Ivan, no."

He turned to grin at her. "Ivan, yes!"

"Ivan, no. Don't start." She shook her head again, mouth arranged into a crooked smile. Her eyes were a bit damp, reddened and puffy from crying, but he'd still made her smile at the end of this terrible, terrible night.

Hiro put on the most exaggerated pleading look he could muster. "Ivan...maybe?"

"I don't understand any of what's going on right now," UberMeta Man informed them both.

Michaela sighed. "It's okay. I do. And Ivan would like to ask, politely, if he can bring you in to test his inventions sometimes." She faced her father. "It wouldn't hurt for you to be around Smallcity some more. Delegate. You could spend more time with, um, with me..." yearning stood out in her tone like a neon sign.

He regarded her with a serious gaze. "I'll consider it," he said. "It could be a valuable measure to keep citizens safe."

Furia looked more cautious than curious about this new idea.

Michaela tilted her head so she could rest it against Hiro's shoulder and sighed. A tired sigh this time, not an exasperated-with-Hiro one.

Their hands were still meshed and he could feel how wonderfully, unexpectedly content she was in this moment. Also exhausted, heartsore, sad, regretful, and anxious but, considering how hard tonight had been on her, that ribbon of happiness outshone them all.

Even so, he almost stopped breathing when she pressed her lips to the side of his neck and whispered, "My hero."

Chapter Thirty One

MICHAELA WOKE IN A rush, switching from *off* to *on* to *threat response* in the time it took to throw her eyelids open. Usually she drifted out of sleep, resenting every inch of drift, but the bed felt wrong, and the sheets were too soft. Her body told her it was past time to get up even though her eyes registered complete darkness.

Her head pounded and her eyes were sore, so she closed them again. Tuesday. She didn't have to work today. But her body still wanted to wake up.

Groaning, she rolled over. Hiro's arm tightened around her waist in a familiar gesture. She cracked one eye open, carefully, and saw the cave which was his bedroom. That explained the too-soft sheets and the darkness.

"Hiro?" she said hoarsely.

"Mmmph?"

He wasn't at his best in the morning. "We have *got* to talk about some colors other than black in here. Charcoal gray, or even light gray, lover. Palettes. We are going to talk about a wonderful thing called *palettes.*"

"Mmmph," he grunted again. It sounded more encouraging than not, though.

"Charcoal gray is nice and gloomy. And we could add some contrasting splashes of yellow, maybe some blue. Light gray, even."

His bicep flexed as he pulled her closer, and his power pushed lightly at her back, moving her inch by slippery inch across satiny sheets until she was snuggled against his warm, bare chest.

"I am a supervillain," he said haughtily, his eyes still closed. "Super. Villain. Supervillains don't use yellow in their lair."

"That should be the title of your autobiography."

He started laughing. She smiled fondly at him until he cracked one eye open, and then she leaned forward to press her curved lips to his.

"I love you, Michaela," he said. "Know why?"

"I—yes, I know. But I'm not sure exactly why."

"I love you because you're so smart. And funny." He whispered a kiss to the edge of her lips. "So powerful." A kiss against her jaw. "Kind, and protective." He kissed her cheek. "Freaking gorgeous." He nibbled his way down the curve of her throat, and her breath hitched.

"Powerful? Really?" Did he think that?

"*UberMeta Man* is afraid of you, Michaela-chan. You made him snap to last night, and I don't think anyone else in the universe can do that," he murmured against her skin and chuckled.

She was caught between wanting to laugh with him and wanting to weep again, remembering last night.

"And you're strong," he told her. "Just about the strongest person I know."

Michaela shifted until she could wiggle an arm under his neck and wrap him tight in her embrace. "I didn't feel all that strong. Until I met you. Then I discovered I can take on anything." She watched his dark hair, a deeper shadow against the surrounding gloom, as he rose over her, caressing her with nothing but his lips and his beautiful words.

"You made it through, Michaela. Years and years of feeling useless, and left out, and lonely. And you still ripped yourself wide open to feel other people's emotions, without complaining about your own. You just did it. You made it through and it would have broken you if you weren't unbreakable. You did that without me because you're made of Titansteel inside where no one saw." He nipped the sensitive place where her neck joined her shoulder, adding yummy shivers to the rest of the feelings swirling around her. "But you'll never have to do it without me again."

"I love you, Hiro."

"I know. I'm super lovable." He lifted his head and pierced her with his cocky grin.

She'd liked that look on him when he was The Evil Bane and she was the Amiable Accomplice tagging along behind Furia like an unwanted toe. She *loved* it, now.

"I'm so glad you hit yourself with your own laser," she blurted. She tugged his left arm closer so she could kiss just below his still-healing, pink scar.

"What?" he snorted.

"So glad. I never would have tried to talk to you unless you came into urgent care. No matter how much I liked looking at you in your Bane mask." She never would have had the guts to defy everything she knew without his stalking in the bushes and flirty conversations and floating flowers. She'd still be locked behind miles and miles of secrets without her Hiro.

"You like the mask? I can go get it." He hooked his thumb over his shoulder and raised his eyebrows.

She laughed. "Not so much the mask as that grin you always had under it. And the jaw. Mmm, this jaw right here. It's killer." She traced her fingers along that chiseled line, reveling in everything, every tiny little circumstance combining to put her here, in this bed, snuggled up with The Evil Bane.

With the skin-to-skin contact, her feelings rushed out of her and into him. She could feel his happiness, the constant thrumming of arousal spiking underneath it. Her power made everything appear drenched in a light mist, gold and pink and dreamy.

"Yeah?" he murmured. "What else do you love about me?" His hands edged underneath the shirt she was wearing, smoothing up the sides of her waist. She'd borrowed it from him to sleep in last night when they'd staggered back inside together, too exhausted to do anything more than undress and tumble into Hiro's king-sized bed.

"Anyone who has a whole room full of his own action figures does *not* need more ego boosting."

"Boost it anyway," he said, smiling.

Under the silly words she could feel the insecurity of the boy who had spent fourteen years without a family, being told he was doing the wrong, Evil things. For that boy she could boost an ego right into the stratosphere.

"I love how protective you are," she said, caressing his hairline. "I love your inventions, you're the smartest person I think I've ever met. I love how protective you are and how much you want to save people." A surge of joy, deliciously warm and peachy bright, shot from him to her and she drank it in. "I really, really love how fearless you are and how you say whatever you want. It's so brave."

"Well, I'm blushing now."

"In that case, your ass is the prettiest thing I've ever had my hands on."

Laughter broke from him as he buried his face against her stomach. "We are going to have so much fun together, my little sidekick." He kissed the curve of her hip, tickling.

"Are we? Let's start now." Deliberately, she sent him a kick of her arousal as she cradled his head against her.

He responded by nibbling his way down the curve of her waist. Like the goofiest actor in a superhero skinflick, he trapped the lace band of her panties between his teeth and pulled them all the way down around her ankles.

It was really unfair how much that cheesy move aroused her.

"You had a hard night," Hiro murmured, and pressed a kiss to the sensitive inside of her thigh. "You just lay there and let me make you feel better."

"Okay," she sighed.

And by the time she'd stopped shaking long enough to untangle her fingers from his hair and he'd kissed his way back up to her lips, Michaela felt better than she had in a long time. Maybe even years.

Still trembling in the aftershocks of her explosive orgasm, she rocked her hips up to press against him.

"Feeling better?" he asked.

"Definitely. So much." She gripped his back and pulled him close, still grateful that she *could* touch him like this. That he would allow it. When he slid inside her, he was even closer, as much a part of her as the rushing of her blood. Sheer happiness leaked out of her in the form of tears, slipping down her temples to tickle her ears, and even that was perfect because Hiro could feel exactly why she was crying and he wasn't worried.

"Love you," he said, his voice rough as he buried his face in the side of her neck and shuddered.

"And I love you," she promised. Her second orgasm rolled over her, slow and intense. She gloried in all of it, the sweet spark of her nerve endings, the sweaty weight of his body over hers, the way he filled up her entire world.

After they'd both caught their breath, Hiro shifted off of her and rolled to his side. He tucked her beside him and Michaela relaxed with her head on his shoulder, ready for some afterglowing.

"So, you're moving into the tower," Hiro said.

"That wasn't a question," she said. "Were you planning to ask?"

"I thought, as my last real supervillain act, I could just kidnap you." Tenderly, he smoothed his free hand up and down her arm.

"It's not kidnapping if I'm helping you move the boxes and adding accent pillows to the bed," she informed him.

"Fine. We'll kidnap Mrs. Fish. I've got three suites up here at the penthouse level and she can pick the one she—why are you giggling?"

Michaela pulled in a deep breath, but she couldn't stop. "I would pay...*real* money..." In, out, in, and she finally had some control over her diaphragm muscles. "I would pay good money to see you try to kidnap Mrs. Fish. Oh, I would love to see that." Poor Hiro wouldn't stand a chance.

"Do you think she'd want to work for E.B. Industries? Something with paperwork or billing or customer service? She can scare any time-wasters away."

Smiling, Michaela shook her head. "Don't even ask. She has a job she loves, in the Neonatal Intensive Care Unit, snuggling preemies. The nurses all know she's an Empath but they're desperate to keep her secret. Mortality in the NICU declined almost twenty percent after she started working there."

"I'm definitely donating to the NICU then. Ask Mrs. Fish what they need."

"But you were being hyperbolic about that 'billionaire philanthropist vigilante' stuff last night. Weren't you?" Michaela asked, peering up at him.

"Ah." Hiro shifted in the bed and squeezed her in a brief half-hug. "Well. Remember I said I created Titanglass and plasteel when I was still working for Technix? I've patented a few other inventions since then. And I bought some properties. Apartment complexes, shopping centers, that kind of thing. E.B Industries manufactures and supplies a lot of materials for construction firms. Which I may also own." His muscles shifted underneath her cheek as he reached up to run his fingers through his hair.

"Not exaggeration, then."

"Nope."

"I'll get a list from Mrs. Fish. And thank you." She squeezed him tight. "You don't know how happy that makes me."

"I do if you want to put your hands on me," he said.

Michaela wiggled her way up to start kissing her supervillain. His neck, his jaw, the soft curve of his smile. He'd just wrapped his other arm around her when they were interrupted by the shrill beep of an alarm.

Hiro groaned and fell back on his pillow. "One morning off with my sexy sidekick and my supervillain costume. Only one. All Powers, was it too much to ask?"

Beeep, Beeep, Beeep.

"Would I be wearing the supervillain costume? Can we get one with leather?" Michaela asked, interested.

Beep, Beep, Beep, the alarm shrieked.

"I would put it up for negotiation." Mumbling and grousing, he crawled to the end of the bed and reached for his gadget-stuffed shirt. The alarm cut off.

Michaela sat up and moved to look at the screen with him. She frowned down at it, not understanding most of the indicator lights.

"Velocity is awake and trying to bust out of his room," Hiro said. "Damn it. He was supposed to be out for at least twelve hours."

She shrugged. "I wouldn't be surprised if his metabolism is accelerated as a side effect of his power."

Hiro narrowed his eyes. "Can I knock him out again?"

"Absolutely not. You're lucky he didn't have any adverse drug reactions from the first dose."

"He *shot at* you," he grumped. "I won't use any tranquilizer. I'll just punch him. He can't react adversely to that."

"I love you, you grouch," she said. "Let's just go talk to him."

"Fine but we are *not* letting him out. I just caught him! I don't want to have to do it again. Maybe we can shut him into the bathroom and let him smell us through the door. That's what they told me to do with Purriarty." He pursed his lips, considering. "You may need to put a hand on him and calm him down a little."

Michaela fought down the chuckles bubbling through her. Giggling would only encourage him. "I'll only touch him if he's actively threatening to hurt us."

Even Chris, a peer she considered a close friend, didn't know about her Empathy. And she didn't like forcing people to feel what she wanted them to feel or sucking out their emotions. She'd get Chris's permission, if it came to that.

Hiro sighed. "Ahhh, scruples. It will be fun getting used to having those again."

She wrapped her arms around him and laid her head on his back. "I'll be here to help. Consider me your conscience, Evil's Bane."

"You're *my* Amiable Accomplice, now," he said. "And I'm never letting you go."

"I'm changing my sidekick name," Michaela told him. "To something superhero-ish. I feel a lot more like a hero, right now." She hugged him again, tight, and then let go to bounce happily over to her pile of clothes. "Let's get dressed and go take care of vigilante business."

EVEN FROM THE OTHER side of the hole in the earth he'd chosen as their battleground Hiro could see Michaela's fierce grin as she dropped to one knee, bent her neck as though at prayer, and waited.

A millisecond later, Captain Champion's shield sliced the air above her nape. Her hair blew out behind it. Then she popped up to run towards their target again, a purple smudge against the rocky walls of the quarry in her sidekick super suit.

It had taken him an embarrassingly long time to catch on to the fact that her super suit was a subtle tribute to her parent's suits. Red and blue, mixed, made purple.

"Alright?" he whispered into the nanoscopic microphone in his suit collar. He'd asked the same thing six times already during the battle and he couldn't make himself *stop* asking even though she was as good at hand-to-hand combat as she'd always been. She'd been on the other side of the fight last time, and it made a huge difference.

Also, she hadn't been dragging his heart around on a leash behind her the last time.

Her voice crackled through his earpiece. "Bane, stop. I'm fine. You know I'm fine." She sent a fist in a wide roundhouse towards the Captain, which of course he ducked. It gave her a chance to sweep her right leg across the backs of his knees.

The superhero stumbled. A puff of powdery quarry dust coated both fighters.

"Bot now," she commanded.

"So bossy," he murmured. "Save it for the bedroom." He tapped the side of his wrist to direct another robot towards Captain Champion's back. It fired a pulse of pure energy, making the superhero stagger again, but Hiro didn't want to incapacitate him. Not until he had enough data to determine how well his bots were performing.

"WHERE IS HE?" the man roared.

"Out of your way, oh Captain, my Captain," Hiro shouted back. "Mwahahaha," he added, as an afterthought.

Michaela's muffled snort echoed through his earpiece.

"Return Veloxity to me now, or I swear I'll bring the entire Legion down on both your heads!" The Captain dodged every shot from Hiro's robot, ducking and rolling like a man half his age. "You'll never be safe again. I'll call Furia and tell her exactly where you are, Amiable Accomplice! I'll let her know of your betrayal." Fury vibrated in every syllable.

Michaela sighed and thrust her foot between his legs while he was mid-duck, sending him sprawling in the dirt.

"Woo! Yeah! Go get him!" From far off to the side, where he was crouched inside their dark, unmarked van, Veloxity cheered for the umpteenth time in Hiro and Michaela's ears.

Worryingly, he wasn't cheering for his Captain Champion.

Michaela turned her head to glare at the van. "Are you *sure* your head felt alright after you woke up, Veloxity? You weren't lying to me?" she asked quietly through their linked earpieces.

They both heard the smile in his voice. "I feel great, Ami. Totally fine. This is awesome."

A huge *BANG* echoed off the rocks, an enormous, flat sound like someone had just dropped a giant's bag of wet metal laundry. One of Bane's drones had blasted the damn shield out of Captain Champion's grip, responding to Hiro's changed battle strategy. The Captain scrambled after it.

Veloxity ducked around the van doors, lifted one fist as high as he could in his chains, and brought it down in an enthusiastic, but silent, pump. He scurried back out of sight.

"Okay he *seemed* totally fine when I checked his vitals this morning," Michaela said. "But I could have missed something. Honey, we need to get a pulse oximeter for the lair."

"As many as you like," Hiro assured her.

He narrowed his eyes, watching the Captain hook his shield back onto his right arm. His suit was also video-recording, which he would review, slow, and dissect thoroughly on his monitors. But his impressions during the actual fight were valid data as well. And he really, *really* needed every bit of information he could get from this fight. He wanted to figure out how to reproduce the indestructible material of the Captain's shield.

This morning, after they'd finally gotten Veloxity calmed enough to listen, they'd explained that The Evil Bane was becoming a vigilante. They told him Michaela was joining his side. Of course Hiro felt like it was a perfectly sensible decision but he had expected at least a *little* pushback from Veloxity.

As soon as they had clarified The Evil Bane, now going by *Evil's Bane*, wanted to arrange a battle with Captain Champion to get data on his mysterious shield, not necessarily to hurt him, Veloxity had been almost scarily enthusiastic about the plan.

"Is there something going on you want to tell me about?" Michaela asked her friend as she darted forward to exchange blows with their target.

"There's *nothing* going on, that's the whole problem." Bitterness bloomed through Veloxity's tone like toxic flowers.

Unrequited feelings would do that to a person. Hiro, sitting safe in the knowledge that Michaela adored him, could even empathize.

"You're...bored?" she panted.

Silence from Veloxity.

"Help me see what the problem is here, my friend. You're acting really strange."

Veloxity fired back, "Stranger than a sidekick becoming a vigilante? How is your Furia going to take that?"

Hiro directed two more bots at the Captain, one at his back, one to try targeting the shield again. Michaela would need some time to digest what he suspected her friend was about to tell her. And anyway he wanted a sample, even a tiny scrape, of the material it was made with. He'd never fought an alloy like it.

"Don't change the subject," Michaela said. She danced back from the lethally spinning disc. Hiro directed a third bot forward. Michaela cleared her throat, tentatively. "Do you, like, want to get out here and help? I mean, he is your superhero."

"Someone needs to convince *Captain* he's my superhero then. Because he sure as all powerless hells doesn't act like he knows that."

"Um." Poor Michaela sounded so confused. For the one with Empathy, she was lagging on this one. Beneath the lights of his mask, Hiro smirked.

"I could be there for him. I *am* there for him," Veloxity said, passionately. A clinking sound echoed into their earpieces. He must be trying to gesture with his confessional monologue. "I could be everything he needs and he keeps pushing me away. He says he wants to keep me safe, but that's not what a sidekick is for. I could care less if I'm safe as long as I'm with him. And then he says it's unprofessional and tells me again how much older he is than me, and he pushes me away *again*."

"Oh. *Ohhh*." Michaela said. She ducked back to Hiro's side. They watched together as Captain Champion leapt, dragged a bot to the dirt, and pounded on it as if the machine had personally insulted his entire family, their goldfish, and all of their topiary. "Veloxity. I'm sorry."

Hiro took the opportunity to send a fourth bot out, trying to scratch a sample from that unscratchable material.

"I hate to say it, but you know the Legion has that conduct rule about superheroes dating their sidekicks, right?" she said sadly.

They didn't have a conduct rule about superheroes dating supervillains, because it had never occurred to anyone that impossibility might happen.

Nothing the bot did would sink even a millimeter through that frustrating material. Hiro directed it to try ultrasonic scans, instead, and listened to the love of his life as she tried to talk sense to his lovesick enemy.

A deep sigh from Veloxity met their ears. "Yeah. I do know about the rule."

Unexpectedly, Michaela laughed. "You should have seen his face in the message he sent Bane this morning. I didn't know he even *had* a webcam and then there was his eight minute message full of shouting and wild eyes and 'if you touch one hair on my sidekick's head I'll rip your kneecaps out' and, wow." She ducked a flying shard of robotic arm.

Captain Champion seemed to be taking out every frustrated feeling he'd ever had on the robot. He ignored the other three bots circling him. He didn't try to shout at them anymore, he didn't even talk. Just let out inarticulate growls. Hiro's scan was returning some *interesting* statistics on the superhero's famous shield.

"Oh yeah? Eight minutes long." Veloxity whistled in an impressed way. "Do you still have it? Can you send it to me?"

"I'll direct it to your personal email right now," Hiro told him, opening another window on his monitor. "Ready for the big rescue? I've got all the data I think I can get."

"Sure thing," Veloxity said. He sounded much more cheerful than he had this morning. "Can you maybe drag me out as a hostage? With a gun to my head? That would be so dramatic."

"I'm liking where you're going with this," Hiro said. "It's been a pleasure working with you. I'm sorry about, you know, drugging and kidnapping you. And stuff. Amiable Accomplice? Can you—"

"I'm on it," Michaela pelted towards the van.

Hiro raised his voice to include Captain Champion in their conversation. "It's been great, Captain, but I'm afraid we must be going," he shouted. "Other appointments, you know." Contrary to his words, he didn't move.

The superhero staggered to his feet, breathing hard. "You *will* return my sidekick to me now or—"

"Or what?" he interjected. He waved one gloved hand languidly through the air. "Sidekicks are so very replaceable. Just get the Smallcity Legion to assign you another one."

"There *is* no other one!" Captain Champion roared. His usually-severe expression had melted away, revealing a flushed, anguished face. His perfect, professional side-part was now a tousled mess of dark brown hair, the salt-and-pepper streaks masked by gritty quarry dust.

Michaela reappeared, dragging Veloxity by the chains wrapped around his torso. She also held something short and stubby to his temple. It took Hiro a second to recognize the thing as a spare piece of PVC pipe from the toolkit in the back of the van.

Veloxity could have released those chains any time he wanted, they'd both shown him the hidden catch above his waist. But maybe he'd been waiting patiently in his chains this entire time for the Captain to shout that one thing, because he couldn't hide the light that hearing it brought to his face.

"Everyone calm down!" Michaela shouted. "We're leaving. We're *all* leaving." She gripped Veloxity tighter and bent close to his ear. Through his earpiece, Hiro heard, "Can I throw you at him?"

Veloxity turned his quick nod into the pretense of trying to jerk away from her. She yanked him back and pushed the innocent piece of pipe harder against his head.

The Captain lifted his trembling arm in front of him and crouched slightly. "Let him go. Let him go *now*."

Hiro didn't want him to toss that dangerous shield at Michaela again. Despite the fact that she trusted in her invulnerability, he didn't know if it had limits. He stepped in front of her and Veloxity. "Perhaps I'm not finished with your sidekick yet. There are so many ways he can assist me, after all."

"Release him now! Don't hide behind my sidekick. Take off that mask, turn off your bots and face me, you coward. You are *nothing* without your tech."

Just for that, Hiro smacked the superhero upside the back of the head with his potenkinesis, watching the man's head jerk forward. He marched towards Captain Champion, waving a hand to indicate Michaela could drag Velocity along behind him. *Say it, you ancient idiot. Say the words for Velocity.* "Why shouldn't I keep him? He's nothing to you, and you know it." Behind his back, he motioned to Michaela.

The Captain's dark eyes caught fire and *burned*. "He is everything to me."

"Now!" Hiro hissed.

Michaela took two quick steps around Hiro and shoved her captive forward so that he crashed into Captain Champion's chest. They hadn't impacted nearly hard enough for the look of agony that etched across the older man's features. He wrapped both arms around his sidekick, chains and all, and gripped him like an anchor in a storm.

Hiro grabbed Michaela's hand and took off for the van. "Got the earpiece back?"

Their feet crunched across the gravel in tandem, their linked hands swung in perfect sync, and his heart felt like it was about to fly out of his chest. Best. Battle. Ever.

"Got it," she said, and tossed him a quick, mischievous smile.

By the time the van doors slammed behind them, they were both cackling. Hiro grabbed the back of her neck and pulled her towards him for a quick, breathless kiss. "You're my sidekick now," he told her. "You're everything to me and I'm smart enough to tell you so. You're the one I love. The one I'm never letting go."

"Plan on it. I'm never going anywhere," she said, smiling at him so bright he wanted to blink. "Now let's go! Back to the lair, Evil's Bane."

THE END

Don't miss out!

Visit the website below and you can sign up to receive emails whenever SE White publishes a new book. There's no charge and no obligation.

https://books2read.com/r/B-A-OZFO-FUSNB

BOOKS 2 READ

Connecting independent readers to independent writers.

Did you love *The Sidekick and The Supervillain*? Then you should read *Beneath Me*[1] by SE White!

Her feelings for her nemesis are her best kept secret.

Marcelline has been in love with the aquatic superhero Water Wonder for years. It's no surprise. Everyone in Ocean City loves him, his sea-blue eyes, and his skintight super suit. He's the perfect hero. He always saves the day.

He's also totally off limits to Marcelline because the person he's saving the day from is **her.**

As The Sea B*tch, ocean villain extraordinaire, she trades banter, sharp wit, and fierce battles with Water Wonder every day. She can live with forever being beneath his status as a non-human looking villain. She's survived loving him this long, right? But a single unguarded

---

1. https://books2read.com/u/3LRZ1M

2. https://books2read.com/u/3LRZ1M

moment in his hidden lair changes everything and suddenly Marcelline is drowning in a sea of terrible hope. What if Water Wonder doesn't mind her having tentacles instead of legs? What if he could see her as something more than just The Sea B*tch?

What if, this time, the villain could live happily ever after?

Beneath Me is a 13,000 word novelette of fluff, unrequited pining, underwater battles, tentacles, and an opinionated pet lobster. Set in a world where superpowers exist, this short story contains zero cheating, no cliffhangers, and a guaranteed HEA. This sweet and steamy romance is intended for mature audiences. Over eighteen only, please.

Read more at https://www.sewhitebooks.com.

Also by SE White

Super Love
The Sidekick and The Supervillain
Beneath Me

Watch for more at https://www.sewhitebooks.com.

About the Author

SE White is an independent author of contemporary SciFi and historical romance. From characters stumbling into love in the wild west of 1870s Nevada, to supervillains falling hard for heroes, to characters running as fast as they can away from their Soulmates in an alternate modern universe, there's something fun for every reader. SE loves writing the quirky, the sarcastic, the fluffy, and all the niche romance tropes leading to a happily ever after. Guaranteed. She lives and writes in Nevada, USA where she enjoys watching probably unhealthy amounts of Great British Bake Off and spending entirely too much time rating alien romance books on #bookstagram.

Read more at https://www.sewhitebooks.com.